I Loved You First

Reena Jacobs

Also by Reena Jacobs

Shadow Cat (The Striped Ones)
Control Freak: Brandon's Story

I Loved You First
Reena Jacobs

Copyright © 2011 by Reena Jacobs

All rights reserved. No part of this book may be used or reproduced in any manner whatsoever without written permission except in the case of brief quotations embodied in critical articles and reviews. For information email Reena Jacobs: reenajacobs@reenajacobs.com

I Loved You First is a work of fiction. Names, characters, places, and incidents either are the product of the author's imagination or are used fictitiously. Any resemblance to actual persons, living or dead, events or locales is entirely coincidental.

www.ReenaJacobs.com

Acknowledgements

Writing a book is like raising a child; it takes an entire village. I've certainly had my fair share of help along the way. As always, my husband has been supportive as ever in my writing ventures. Though he's not a fan of fiction, he's readily available to lend an ear. Special thanks to Hollie Westring, who beta read. She played a pivotal role in some of the changes made to the final draft. *I Loved You First* is definitely a smoother read because of her help. As many know, I attempted a Kickstarter campaign to raise funds for editing. That was a struggle in itself. Dave Parker, president of my local PFLAG chapter in NC, stepped forward and offered his editing services free of charge. Thank you so much. Special shout out and thanks to Steadman for allowing me to use a few lyrics from their song Come On. Finally, I want to thank those who supported my Kickstarter project through pledges and spreading the word.

Chapter 1

The music blared throughout the house at full blast—Pretty People by Dexter Freebish. Yep, that pretty much summed it up. They surrounded me. Only thing, I didn't want to be like them. Sometimes I was just so tired of the games the so-called "pretty people" played. Yet here I was, the girl hiding in a corner, decorating a wall.

The party was in full swing. Already people had consumed enough alcohol to loosen inhibitions but not enough to send them puking over the balcony. It'd get there though. I'd been to enough of these parties to know it was only a matter of time.

Through the mass of bodies, I could just make out the guys in the kitchen guzzling beer bongs. A few of the more slutty chicks hung off to the side laughing and cheering them on. Once in a while, one of the braver girls joined in and made a mess of her outfit.

The whole thing was stupid, and they'd certainly regret it in the morning.

So why was I here?

The answer pushed through the crowd—my best friend, Seth. BFF since I'd saved him from a beat down in the first grade. Well, actually, I'd bitten the girl's arm who'd bullied him. Nothing like a nip to send a kid crying. I'd gotten in trouble but earned a forever friend in the process. Totally worth it.

Seth chatted to random frat boys as he made his way to me. He was one of the "pretty people." Sandy blond hair, blue eyes, six foot, and a rising star on the baseball team—he was what girls wanted, and he knew it.

I, on the other hand, was just his sidekick. Nearly invisible. I didn't mind so much. It was the same role I'd played in high school. Why should college be any different? He got me into all the good parties I'd preferred to avoid, and I stood by his side as his gossip buddy.

"Here, Alex." Seth pressed a plastic cup of frothy something into my hand. "This is great, huh?"

I shrugged. "Yeah, I guess."

He grinned a toothpaste smile and punched me lightly on the shoulder. "You're such a party crasher."

No. I would just rather be anywhere but here. I took a sip of my urine colored drink, wishing it were a soda instead.

"Oh great. Here comes Cheyenne." Seth downed his drink like he needed fortification. No doubt he did. His Adam's apple bobbed with each gulp, like a buoy on the waves. He took one look at his empty cup then at my full one. I handed it to him, not sure why I took the first taste anyway. After all, I was the DD.

"Thanks." He wiped his mouth with the back of his hand and leaned close, whispering in my ear. "I wish she'd just leave me the hell alone."

I dittoed his sentiments exactly—but for different reasons. My best friend was more than just a best friend to me. Three words summed it up: I heart him. I'd never tell him though. I wasn't stupid. Besides, what he'd told no one but me was a little something I wished I could forget... or ignore. He was gay. Gay wouldn't be bad if I wasn't so in love with him. Now it was just cruel.

Of course that didn't stop him from playing the dating game. Oh no. He was all into burning through the girls. After all, we couldn't have our All American Jock batting for the other team.

I felt for him; I really did. But at the same time, I was bitter. Yeah, I admit it. It hurt watching him with other girls, wishing it was me instead. I wanted him for myself but knew I'd never have him. So, I settled for the next best thing—being by his side... being the one he shared his hopes and dreams with. What more could a girl in love ask for?

Cheyenne Gordon—cheerleader extraordinaire stepped up to the plate with her personal entourage and created a semi-circle around us. It didn't matter she was a third-year student and we were only freshmen. Young. Old. Every girl wanted a little "sumpin sumpin" with Seth.

She gave me a cursory glance before turning her attentions to my buddy.

Like I said, sidekick. Worthy of notice, but not that much. I blended into the background, the official fly on the wall. Times like this I felt like nothing more than Seth's mascot.

"Hey, Cheyenne." Seth gave her the full smile. I'd told him a million times he should major in drama. He really did have talent. I hadn't even known about his little secret until he'd told me in ninth grade. By then, the girls had started to take notice of his beach boy looks. I guess my best friend just couldn't take the pressure of impersonating straight folks and had to get it off his back.

We'd talked about him coming out of the closet, but in reality we both knew pigs would fly first. He couldn't even bring himself to tell his father. I understood in a way. His dad, Brandon Richards, was everything Seth wanted to be. Mr. Richards really was a great dad—never missed a school event. Even I'd hate to disappoint him. Then again, considering how supportive the guy was, I doubt Seth had much to worry about. But then it was Seth's secret to share and mine to keep for him.

Talking to Cheyenne, Seth made all the right moves. A nod at the appropriate moment, a quick peek at her near non-existent breasts, then the hand on her hip.

I knew the routine, but those touches belonged to me. Hadn't I waited long enough? My only consolation was the fact it'd all lead to nothing. He'd probably date her—for appearance sake. It'd last for a few weeks—longer if things stayed platonic. When it turned serious, he'd brush her off like dirt on his jersey after a home run. Yesterday's old news. It was the way things always played out.

Cheyenne twirled her dull brown hair around her fingers. I knew the girl thought she was cute. But really, my hair was better with the deep brown waves kissed by the sun. Genetics—a combination of a black mom and white dad gave me kickass hair. Of course no one would ever know since I kept it in a single braid going down my back. I'd learned at an early age people couldn't keep their hands to themselves. If I let my hair loose, they were all over it. If I could ever find my voice, I'd scream, *respect the bubble*.

My mom was convinced one day everyone would be like me—dark hair, olive skin.

"So you wanna get something to eat?" Cheyenne stepped closer, bringing her body flush with Seth's. I envisioned myself snatching her away by her scraggy hair.

Seth looked at me. "Alex?"

All eyes drifted my way.

"I guess." *Bummer.* My voice squeaked. Heat spread through my body, concentrating on my face and chest.

"Alright. Let's go." Seth set the empty cups in a nearby planter.

"Well..." Cheyenne looked at me, hesitation written all over her face. "We kinda don't have room for everyone."

Quick tally—Seth, Cheyenne, her three groupies, and me. Unless she had a mini-van—

"That's okay. I brought my bike." Seth nodded to the helmets I guarded—another one of my invisible girl lackey chores. "We'll meet you there."

Cheyenne bit her lip, and I could see the wheels turning in her mini-brain. She pouted. "Fine."

I tried to hold back a grin. I thought I succeeded until Cheyenne frowned at me. Okay, maybe my lips curled a little. But really, I could be happy over little things, right?

Cheyenne turned to Seth and found her smile again. "Gretel's, okay?"

A shrug from me and Seth said, "Sure."

"Great." Cheyenne left, taking team cheerleader with her.

Seth took a deep breath and released it. "Let's do this thing."

As glad as I was to escape the crowd of funky bodies, I couldn't keep my mouth shut. "I don't know why you always go along. You could say no, you know."

The are-we-really-going-to-get-into-it-now look Seth gave was all I needed to drop the matter, at least for now.

On our way out, Bruce Derrick stopped Seth on the porch with a slide of the hand and knuckle bump. "'Sup, dude."

"Heading to Gretel's. Wanna join?" My friend knew how to play it cool. Seth had never told me, but I wasn't fooled. He had a secret crush on Bruce. I saw it in the stray glances, the look of longing for something just out of reach; the same kind I probably gave my good buddy when he wasn't watching. Yeah. I got that. Totally.

Bruce would probably kick Seth's ass, if he got a whiff. He could do it too.

The guy was at least six-three and ripped. I'd seen him enough times without his shirt to know.

Seth was big into dragging me to Bruce's football practices. His excuse—he liked football, and freshmen couldn't try out for sports at Van Buren University, so he might as well enjoy his time in the bleachers while he had the chance.

Yeah, whatever. We'd never gone to the football practices in high school. So what changed? Simple—Bruce wasn't a showcase in our school. Not being into football and all, my best guess was the guy was a receiver or something.

Bruce planted a hand on Seth's shoulder and leaned close as if bestowing a great secret. Bruce's dark hair mixed with Seth's light. God how I wished Seth would get in close with me like that. "Look, I can put in a good word for you to coach. I've seen you toss a pretty good ball, you can run, catch. He might let you try out for the team if you can get in some practice, bulk up a little."

"I don't know. Baseball's my thing." Seth actually flushed as he gave a shy grin.

After all these years, I should have been immune. But really, he was just too yummy. I yearned to rest my head against his chest and run my fingers through the soft hair at the nape of his neck.

"Think about it, man." Bruce slapped Seth on the shoulder. "See ya."

Seth stood entranced as Bruce walked off. The boy had it hard. Though the football stud was too bulky for me, I could see the appeal he might have for Seth.

At five-one, I was still clawing my way to one hundred pounds. Seth was more than enough for me. I knew from the hugs I'd snuck here and there, that I fit comfortably in my buddies arms. No doubt, he'd want a guy who could do the same for him—a guy like Bruce. I couldn't blame him really, not when it felt so good.

"Come on. Let's go." I didn't wait for Seth to follow as I headed to his Kawasaki.

It was obvious Mr. Googly-Eyes needed a little time to get over his crush. That was fine. I could wait. The longer we wasted here, the less time I had to spend with Cheerleader Cheyenne. I pulled my helmet on, loving the snug fit, and swung my leg over the seat.

Alright. Enough was enough. My boy might be able to pass the love-struck look for deep thought. But if he kept it up, eventually someone would catch on to his little secret.

I snapped my fingers and held out a hand. "Keys."

Seth moped over, dropped them in my palm, and got on behind.

I loved when he road bitch. The warmth of his body pressed tight against my back, his hands around my middle. Yeah—this was the life. I should have felt bad about taking pleasure in something meant to be innocent, but I was too busy loving it to care. Seth laid his chin on my shoulder. We'd probably beat the cheer squad to the diner—the benefits of being able to weave through the cars on a motorcycle.

I took off with a jerk. Seth hated when I did that, but it forced him to grip me even tighter. He scooted forward with his thighs encasing mine, and his groin pressed against my butt. I smiled as we left the college scene behind and headed toward the city.

Chapter 2

Motorcycle magazine in hand, I flopped on Seth's bed.

My position gave me a direct line of sight to my friend in his bathroom. Every student received their own personal suite with a private bath, small living room, and miniature kitchen which included a microwave and fridge. No stove. Administration didn't trust young college students to not burn down the dorm. Campus living—one of the many perks of attending Van Buren University.

I set the magazine aside and shook my head at Seth's primping. "I don't know why you do this to yourself."

"Like I have a choice." He raked a comb through his hair, giving the reflection in the mirror his full concentration. He always avoided gels, leaving his hair baby soft. On rare occasions, I ruffled my fingers through the silky strands. I'd always pretended like it was in play, but really I just loved the texture.

"I don't have time for this." He slammed the comb down and tousled his hair, substituting the neat and tidy look for unkempt bad boy and turned to me. "How's this?"

I pinched my chin, going for serious. Black loafers—*nice*. Tight black jeans—*oh, double nice!* Blue shirt which contrasted perfectly with his eyes. The effect had me saying *nom nom nom* inside. I shrugged. "It's okay, I guess."

He narrowed his eyes then turned back to the mirror and fluffed his hair a bit more. "Yeah. I guess you're right. Okay it'll have to do. Let's go."

I puffed a breath of air. "Here we go again."

"Just come on."

As if I had any other choice when he grabbed his jacket on the way to the door, leaving me to lock up.

Seth's first date with Cheyenne was tonight. Well, kinda date, that was. After all, I was along for the ride. *Lame.* "This third wheel bull really needs to stop, Seth."

"You know good and well you're not the third wheel. If anyone is, it's Cheyenne. Why can't you just play along?"

Because I love you. "Because it's just not right to lead folks on."

He stopped in his tracks. "Out here, Alex? Is this where we're doing it?"

I looked down the not-so-empty hall of the dorm. Wrong time, wrong place. Still didn't make it right.

"What would you have me do then?" His voice bled all sorts of huffy.

I rolled my eyes so hard, my mama would have slapped them straight if she'd seen. "Nothing... I guess."

He gave me a wild-eyed stare. I don't know what he was trying to pull, but I hated that look. He only did it when he was angry, like he was psycho or something. Freaky. If it were anyone but Seth, I'd run for my life. Instead, I locked eyes with him, refusing to back down.

Like always, he broke contact first. "Whatever. We're already going to be late."

Score: Alex - 1, Seth - 0.

"Fine." A temporary truce for now, because I certainly wasn't finished.

We hoofed it to Cheyenne's sorority—the Pi Phi Alpha house—and stepped up to the door. And that was it; we just stood, wasting time.

"Well? Are you going to knock?" I asked.

"Yeah." Seth shifted from side to side then rubbed his hands on his pants.

What was with the antsy bit? It wasn't as if it were his first fake date. Then it hit me. It had little to do with Cheyenne and a lot to do with Bruce.

Before football practice, Bruce suggested Seth meet up for some darts. With Cheyenne hanging about and conveniently inviting herself, Seth had no choice but to make it a date.

I couldn't help but take pity on him. "Chill. You're making *me* nervous." I reached past him and rapped the knocker.

Footsteps tumbled down the stairs, and the door flew wide open, revealing a breathless Cheyenne. With the slight flush on her face, she looked pretty good, sexy even. *Bitch*.

"Ready?" Seth threw on his winning smile.

"Yeah," she gushed all airy and crap. *The faker*. As head cheerleader, she was at the top of her game. No way would a short dash down the stairs leave her winded. She disappeared to the side and returned with a coat in hand.

Seth made an obvious play of checking her out from head to toe, while I shoved my hands in my pocket so they didn't reach out and thump my little star actor in the back of the head.

"You look nice," he said.

Cheyenne beamed." You too."

Seth was right, the girl did look nice. Better than nice. She looked fantastic! The shiny lavender blouse was the perfect shade to bring out the highlights in her normally plain brown hair. But it was the snug khaki pants in calf-high boots which set the outfit. I hoped she'd embarrass herself with camel toe this evening.

Despite the urge to growl and yell, *mine*! I turned tail and tramped toward the college activity center like the coward I was. Seth didn't need me to coach him on how to make nice with his soon-to-be girlfriend, and no way did I want to see it. Instead I kept point and did my best to tune out Seth's low murmurs and Cheyenne's grating laugh echoing behind me.

I picked up the pace, trying to distance myself from her annoying giggles. Shoes slapped against the pavement behind me, but I stayed the course.

"Hey, Alex. Wait up, will you?" Seth called.

Like a trained dog, I froze in place.

He circled to my front and placed a hand on my shoulder. Through my light jacket, the warmth of his touch spread through my body like a slow burn. Seth leaned in. He drew so close, his breath tickled my ear, and the scent of his aftershave washed over me—a masculine mixture of fresh cut wood and spice. I forced myself to look forward and not turn my head so our lips would brush.

"Come on. I need you here," he whispered while looking back at Cheyenne.

Why couldn't he have left me in my dorm? Right now, I hated him and the torture he put me through. But I loved him too much to resist even one of his requests. "Yeah. Okay."

"Thanks." He pulled back and gazed into my eyes until I was sure I'd melt on the spot. "You're the greatest. I mean that, you know."

I smiled and looked away. "Yeah. I know."

"Great." He released his hold and gave me a playful punch on my cooling shoulder. "Now let's do this thing."

Cheyenne caught up and we walked the rest of the way in silence. I couldn't help but notice the occasional resentful look she passed my way, but what did I care? She'd be out of the picture in no time.

On campus and open until ten o'clock, the activity center—AKA Johnson Hall—was a regular hangout spot on the weekdays. Thanks to some band, tonight it was packed. Not an empty seat in sight.

"I think I see him," Seth said.

I craned my neck to catch a glimpse over the multitude, but the best I could do was take the measurements of people's backs and stomachs. I took

Seth's word and crowded behind Cheyenne as he pushed through. Her fruity aroma tickled my nose. Quite delicious, really. If it weren't for the fact she'd be hanging all over my BFF tonight and getting her tasty scent all over him, I'd ask her to share the name of her fragrance. As it were, all I could think about was her marking my territory.

The crowd disbursed the further away we got from the entrance. We bypassed the eating area filled with people laughing and talking with their mouths full and reached the game room. I stopped at the threshold. Forget about finding a pool table. Stacks of quarters lined rails as people waited for their turns to play the winner. Usually there was enough to go around. Not tonight with the band and all. But that wasn't our destination.

"Bruce," Seth called.

The big guy turned around, dart in hand, and grinned. "Thought you weren't going to make it."

"Just had to make a quick stop first." Seth wrapped an arm around Cheyenne and brought her to the forefront, leaving me behind.

Guess I'm just a nobody. Big surprise there.

Bruce cocked his head and gave a wink. "Gotcha." He returned his attention to the dartboard and took aim before launching his mini missile. It hit the cork with a thunk, right in the outer five ring.

Bruce laughed. "Did I mention I've only played a few times?"

"At least you hit it." Seth clapped hands with Bruce while I found a discrete corner where I could fade away.

I should have brought a book.

"You met the guys on the team." Bruce stood at a right angle to Seth, opening the conversation to others.

Two players I recognized from the field stepped forward. Bruce was big, but these guys were Goliaths—not just tall, but meaty. If Dwayne Johnson was The Rock, these guys were The Mountains. They towered over Seth like Seth towered over me. Did it make him feel as insignificant as I felt most of the time?

Seth passed handshakes all around, and a few knuckle bumps to spare. "Yeah, man. Bill and Dink."

Which one was which, I didn't know. The smaller of the two—if smaller could be applied to guys like this—had blond hair. The other? Hair as dark as night.

"Even number. We can play teams now." Bruce handed each guy one dart. "Ones with the closest and furthest from the bulls-eye are partners."

Seth held Cheyenne's arms in the semblance of an intimate moment, and his pelvis tilted toward hers as he looked into her eyes. "Do you mind?"

Hell yeah, I minded. Not that anyone cared but me.

Cheyenne shook her head with a smile. Apparently, the gal knew her role—The Trophy.

"Alright." Seth threw me a nod before taking his place with the boys.

Bill and Dink were the experience two, each hitting inside the center ring with the raven-haired one almost hitting the bulls-eye. Seth threw last, and the dart bounced off the board, impaling the floor. Two additional throws and he got one to stick.

Goliath the Larger retrieved the darts. "Five-oh-one, okay?"

"We'll explain as we go," Goliath the Smaller said with a voice as deep as he was tall. He held up a pad. "Who's keeping score?"

"You want to, Alex?" Seth asked.

Four pairs of eyes hit as if seeing me for the first time. If there was anything I hated more than being ignored, it was being the center of attention. Though I wanted nothing more than to ghost away, I emerged from my shadowy corner. One foot in front of the other, it took forever to reach the tall blond with everyone scrutinizing each step. Up close, his size stunned me. Yeah I was short, but for the first time since I'd reached my full height, I felt like a toddler.

"Here. Let me." Blondie scrambled for a chair and set it out of the way before returning to me. His meaty hand encompassed the entire width of my arm as he pulled me along like a child. At his physical direction, I dropped in the chair.

He took a knee and passed me the pad with the names already written in the Home and Away Team slots. Bill and Seth versus Dink and Bruce. He pushed a pencil in my hand and explained the rules of the game, not once looking up as his thick finger trailed the paper.

I tried to pay attention, really I did, but his explanations were so disorganized my mind wandered.

Not at all like my golden boy friend, the giant's locks had a red undertone. On a girl, I'd dub it strawberry blond. Did guys use that term for themselves?

"Got it?" He lifted his head revealing thick lashes surrounding green eyes with golden starburst centers. As close as he was, I could count each and every one of the freckles splattered across his nose.

Not in the least. "Maybe with a little coaching."

He smiled which planted a dimple in his right cheek. Adorable baby cute came to mind, but with his size, comparing him to an infant was an oxymoron if ever there was one. "Here. We'll just tell you what to subtract. Can you do that?"

"Sure."

"Good." He rubbed my thigh a bit too rigorously before huddling with Bruce.

I checked the score pad.

Away Team: Dink and Bruce

A name for the lumbering blond. That made the dark one Bill.

I lost track of time as the guys played game after game.

Cheyenne started strong, even going as far as to cheer Seth on, though my homeboy sucked at darts. Eventually her patience wore thin.

I didn't blame her. There was only so long a gal could sit on the sidelines watching the guy she was with ignore her on a date. Even at sport events she had her fellow cheerleaders by her side for entertainment. Here she had no one.

Being the sidekick and all, I'd long since learned to get over boredom. I kept myself busy by dissecting people. *People watching* was the name I'd given it. Other than spending time with Seth, it was my next favorite thing to do and the main reason I decided on a sociology major.

A girl like Cheyenne probably spent more time watching herself than others. She put her hand to her mouth and stifled a yawn. A quick glance at the clock on the wall, and she approached Seth from behind, snaking her arms around his waist. "I'm about ready to go."

"Sure thing. I'll see you on the field." He didn't even glance her way.

Cheyenne winced, and I perked up.

Seth, usually so good at lavishing girls with attention, disentangled her arms and retrieved the darts. "I'm up."

"Seth," she whined. "It's dark out there."

My buddy's hand froze with the dart set for release. *Tick. Tock. Tick. Tock.* I could only imagine what was going through his mind. Whatever it was, he took too long to work through it.

"Seth?" The annoyance in her voice was enough to snap anyone out of deep thought.

"The center's closing in about half an hour anyway." Bruce came to the rescue. "We can play another time."

"Yeah. Okay." Seth's eyes lingered on Bruce. "Another time." He passed the darts to Bill. "Good game."

"I can take Alex home," Dink said.

"That'd be great," Cheyenne chimed with a mischievous smile.

"No." A little too hasty, Seth could at least pretended like he was thinking about it. He had no problem mulling over things a few seconds ago.

Cheyenne's smile dropped like it'd never been.

"I mean. It wouldn't be right to pass Alex off when I brought her." Seth didn't meet anyone's gaze as he grabbed Cheyenne's coat and held it open.

All I could do was shake my head. Not only was the damage already done, but that was the lamest excuse I'd ever heard pass through his lips. Even I wanted to slap the piss out of him.

"Can we go now?" Cheyenne's mouth twisted, and she gave me a contemplative look I'd like to call 'revenge will be sweet with you.'

"Sure."

Thanks for screwing us both, Seth. I stood, and Dink was at my side with a jacket in hand. I stared at it for a full second, not recognizing it. When I realized it was mine, I looked up, up, up at him and met his sheepish grin. He shrugged, and I hoped the heat spreading throughout my body and tingling my scalp didn't color my face red. Surprise. Confusion. Whatever was happening right now was beyond my understanding. So, I did the only thing I could think to do. I gave him my back.

Like a pro, he slid my jacket up my arms like he'd performed the move a million and one times.

"Thanks." I couldn't bring myself to look him in the eyes. Instead, I took my spot next to Seth.

Fitting the band would be singing Come on by Steadman—*If your heart is beating, it don't mean that you're alive. If you don't try, then I'll see you on the other side*—as we left.

My heart was jack hammering after my brief encounter with Dink. Yet living in Seth's shadow I didn't feel much alive. In fact, fake was more like it. How could I expect Seth to come out, when I couldn't bring myself to share my feelings with him?

We walked Cheyenne back to her sorority in virtual silence. Irritation radiated off her like a gnat buzzing in the ear. No peck on the cheek at the door. Not even a quiet goodbye. Just the slow close of the door and a disappointed shake of her head.

The fake romance was over before it had even started, and Seth was mine again. Only thing, I didn't feel like the winner. *If you don't try.* Try? Try?! No one knew Seth like I did, yet I didn't have a shot. Trying to make him love me the way I loved him was as futile as Cheyenne's attempt at dating him.

Seth gave a weary sigh and faced me. No doubt he was thinking of his next steps: repair the relationship with Cheyenne or find a new temporary girlfriend. "Well? My dorm or yours?"

"Yours," I said.

"So be it."

Side by side, we cut across campus. Where to go wasn't difficult for me to decide. If I'd said mine, Seth would have left as the night wore on. Choosing his meant I could feign tired at any time, taking my place beside him, curling in his arms. Already I envisioned the warmth of his body despite the coolness of the air filtering through my light coat.

Eventually thoughts of Cheyenne intruded, sapping the cozy warmth I'd built. Cheerleader Bimbo didn't seem like the type to let a slight go. Some people were like that. One of the many unpleasantries of life. Why did Seth have to choose her? Even one of the drones from Team Cheer would have been better than the queen herself.

And how Seth—mister suave—could screw up so royally was a mystery in itself. Sure, my boy had the hots for Bruce, but that shouldn't have fried half my buddy's brain cells.

"So, I'm wondering," I began, trying to form an intelligent question from my scattered thoughts. "How are you going to handle the Cheyenne situation?"

Seth continued in silence. If I didn't know him so well, I'd think he was ignoring me. But having a connection closer to him than anyone else in my life, I took his silence as deep thought.

I loved and hated that part of Seth. The answers he provided after a quiet were usually well-constructed and logical. I appreciated his sensibility. Yet, I wanted immediate answers. Why did it take a minute or two to come up with a response? I didn't care what anyone said; sixty seconds was an eternity. I'd stood in front of the microwave enough times, waiting for snacks to know.

My mother called it the "now syndrome." I called it just being reasonable.

By the time he answered, we had reached his dorm. "I'll let her make the next move."

My hope sank like a dip on a rollercoaster. "Cheyenne is too high maintenance. I say go for a clean break. Perhaps someone different would be better." *Like me.*

"Maybe." He opened the door and let me pass. "I want to show you something."

Giddiness became me. Seth always had the best surprises.

Instead of taking the stairs to his room, he opened a side door and started up the steps. Personally, I'd done enough walking for the evening. But forever the jock, Seth preferred to forego the elevators whenever he deemed reasonable. *Can always use the extra exercise,* he'd say like he was my father trying to lose a few extra pounds. Like always, I was along for the ride.

After too many flights, he pushed open the door at the top, letting in a cool breeze. I walked onto the rooftop and took in the scene. High enough to see over most of the campus buildings, the New York City lights flickered back at me. I turned to Seth.

In a crouch, he propped the door open with a rock. "It locks from the other side."

Seth walked to me and took me by the hand. Warmth radiated up my arm, sending tingles straight to my heart and a smile to my face.

"This is what I wanted to show you." He led me to the edge of the roof, the cement guard the only barrier to a deadly fall.

My stomach plummeted as I tried to convince my head I wasn't going over the side.

"I found this place the first week we arrived," Seth said. "I love it."

He leaned over the edge, and I forced myself not to grab and scold him like a mother saving a child heading into the street.

"Up here, I can pretend I'm already on my way to Alpha Centauri." Seth, the astronaut and visionary. Despite the slow advances in space travel, my buddy still believed we'd make it outside the solar system in our lifetime. He hopped atop the guard.

"Seth!" My heart fluttered as vertigo hit.

He looked down at me, held out his hand. "Join me, Wendy. A few happy thoughts and you too can fly."

"No way. Wendy got a dose of fairy juice."

Seth smiled. "Dust, Alex. It was dust."

"Whatever. You won't catch me up there in this lifetime."

He faced forward and spread his arms. The wind caressed his blond hair as he tilted his head back. Spectacular was the word which came to mind—like the Greek god Hermes ready to take flight. I loved him all the more for his strength... his courage. If only I was the goddess to stand by his side instead of a shadow beneath his wings.

Chapter 3

"I wish she'd stop looking over here." I flicked a black bug which had crept near me off the bleachers. God I hated the creepy crawlies.

Seth glanced at Cheyenne who was chatting with the other cheerleaders on the field and shrugged. "You wouldn't know she was looking if you weren't looking too."

"That's silly. Now you sound like my mother."

Cheyenne pulled her hair out of a scrunchie and flipped the raggedy brown mess over her shoulder before tying it back again. I couldn't hear her, but I could see her lips moving. Then she tilted her head back and laughed with the cheer squad following suit.

"What do you think she's saying?" I asked.

"Probably: I wish Alex would stop looking over here." Seth chuckled.

"Come on." I pushed him. "I doubt she even knows my name. Really. What do you think they're talking about?"

"What does it matter?" He returned his attention to the football team.

I pictured his muscled thighs and firm butt in the tight football pants and grew hot. The crack and clatter of protective gear startled me out of my forbidden thoughts, and I looked at the field just in time to see a giant of a linebacker ram the quarterback from the side.

Seth hissed air through his teeth. "Yikes. That's gotta hurt."

The thought of my buddy getting pummeled like that left a hollowed sensation in the pit of my stomach. "Are you really thinking about trying out next season?"

"Maybe."

"Why? You don't have time for baseball *and* football."

Silence greeted me.

"They just started tryouts for baseball this week. The football games are happening *right... now*. They overlap, Seth." Sure, baseball practices were in the afternoon while the football team worked out in the morning. But still, that was a lot to handle when we still had to make the grade. I turned to him.

Seth's jaw was tight enough to snap but didn't twitch a millimeter. Great. Now I was stuck with the granite buddy.

"You don't even play football." I plopped my arms against my chest but unfolded them when I realized it could be construed as pouting. The last thing I wanted was for Seth to look at me and think his friend had turned into a whiny Cheyenne doppleganger.

It was just like my buddy to clam up when he didn't want to talk about something. When would he learn? Not talking wouldn't make the problems go away. I waited out the silence as long as I could. "Seth?"

"Will you just drop it, Alex?"

"Uhm. No."

He gave an audible sigh. "Oh my *god!* You're worse than Sarena."

Ouch. Being compared to his twelve-year-old sister definitely was not the effect I was trying for. His irritation irritated me. Seth dragged me out here, not the other way around. If anyone should be in a pissy mood, it should be me. I brooded in silence, thinking about his reason for considering football along with his not so secret crush. I'd even convinced myself he'd tell me in time, and it wasn't my place to bring it up. And then... "I know you have a thing for Bruce."

The slight tension in his body relaxed before most people would have caught it. Being his best friend and all, it was like having a thousand arrows pointing his way.

I bumped him shoulder to shoulder. "Oh please. There's no way you could have kept something like that from me."

Seth stared straight ahead as if I weren't even there. The skeleton in biology class would have been more responsive.

This time I rammed him hard enough to topple him to the side. "What's your problem?"

"Just drop it, okay?"

"Fine. Just so you know: I've known since you first fluttered your eyes at him."

"Alex!"

Finally a response and one which put me one up, at that. I couldn't hold back my laughter as I mentally checked the scoreboard under my name.

The coach gave his bullhorn one long blare before yelling into it. "Alright, ballerinas! Hit the shower."

The sigh of relief the players released traveled all the way to the bleachers. The coach had worked them so hard they didn't even try to jog to the locker rooms. Heads bowed, they trudged off the field.

I lifted an eyebrow. "And you think you can do football *and* baseball? Oh please."

A lone figure broke from the herd of players—number fifty-two. He found energy from somewhere and drew his shoulders back while notching his chin up a couple of inches. He tried to pull off easy strides, but the slight limp ruined the effect. That and the fact I'd just seen the coach work the team into a pile of quivering jelly.

Number fifty-two reached the front bleachers, pulled off his helmet, and shook out blondish red hair darkened with sweat. Dink. A weary smile played on his lips. "Hey, Alex. Hey, Seth."

That was a first. Most people didn't even realize I existed, much less knew my name. Like a dummy, I sat there mute, waiting for someone to move my lips.

Thankfully, Seth didn't need a ventriloquist. "What's up?"

"Informal rush week—upper classmen only." Mischief was written all over Dink's face as he wagged his eyebrows and flexed the dimple in his right cheek. "You can't pledge until spring, but you can sure as hell enjoy the parties. You in?"

Seth glanced at the players disappearing into the gym. Bruce stood at the entrance of the building and waved his helmet over his head before heading inside. With the man of Seth's dreams out of sight, my boy returned his attention to Dink. "Yeah sure."

The titan focused his eyes on me. "Alex?"

I jumped at my name but couldn't formulate a thought other than, Alex what?

The silence drew out, and his grin widened. "Well? You coming?"

I was the deer; his eyes were the headlights.

"Yeah, she's coming," Seth answered.

"Great. Stop by Saturday night, any time after eight." He tapped his helmet on the metal bleachers. "I'll see you there."

"Wait. Your fraternity is co-ed?" That I'd found my voice even surprised me.

"No." Dink laughed a deep sound which matched his voice and size. "But a party with just guys is well... gay."

I forced myself not to look my friend's way. *Bruce and Seth. Party of two. Paging Bruce and Seth. Party of two.* "I guess."

Dink backed away, aiming his helmet at us. "Don't stand me up. Alpha Epsilon."

"After eight," Seth called.

"Right." Dink turned around, jogged to the building, and disappeared inside.

With the football players gone, the only ones left were the cheerleaders practicing on the sidelines. Their pyramid was crap. I could have sworn those were old school, anyway. "I wonder if Cheyenne will be there."

"Who cares?!" Seth stood and stomped down the bleachers.

I hopped after him and tugged his pants at the butt crack.

He twirled around and slapped my hand. "What are you doing?

We'd just learned about universal facial expressions in psychology this week. If he were on the test, I'd choose anger for the furrowed brows and surprise for the o-shaped mouth. I laughed through my explanation. "Your panties seemed bunched, and I thought I'd help."

The surprise faded leaving behind livid outrage. Without a word, he turned and walked away.

I chased after. "Wait. Where are you going?"

"Away from you."

"I was just kidding." I grabbed his arm, and he jerked out of my hold. "What's wrong? Is it the Bruce thing?"

"Will you get over it, already?"

"I doubt Bruce is gay."

He stopped and towered over me. Not just stood in front, but really loomed, crowding my space. He grabbed my arm, looking down his nose. "Don't you think I know that?"

His voice was a hushed whisper between his teeth. I'd never felt so intimidated in my life.

Seth released me and took a deep breath. "I need some time to myself. I'll stop by your room in a couple of hours, and we'll head to the frat house."

"Don't you think we should talk about it?"

"Don't you get it? I don't want to talk." He ran his fingers through his golden hair. "Look. Just because you can't stop rambling doesn't mean I have to listen. I'll catch you later."

His long stride took him down the length of the field at an accelerated pace. No way could I keep up without jogging beside him like an idiot. So, I stood helpless as he left me behind. In no time at all, he disappeared around a corner.

I turned back to the cheerleaders practicing. Cheyenne watched me as the other girls cheered around her. I couldn't see the details of Cheyenne's face at my distance, but I imagined if I could, her expression would be joy.

♥

A light knock woke me. I turned over, letting the radio lull me back to sleep. It wasn't as if I had anything better to do with my best friend ditching me. Another rap on the door, this time a little louder.

I pulled myself to the headboard and let my cotton-stuffed head roll on my neck. "Yeah?"

The door swung open, and Seth poked his head in. "Ready?"

Late afternoon naps were the worst. I swear it sapped every ounce of motivation from my body. I checked the clock, and it blipped eight thirty-seven. *Ready? If by ready you mean turn in for the night, sure.* I planted my feet on the floor and buried my head in my hands. "I guess."

Seth closed the door behind him and sat next to me. "Sorry I went emo on you."

"I shouldn't have nagged. I knew you were upset when I started." I pulled my shoulder blades back, stretching my chest then touched my elbows to loosen my back. Not the slightest bit eager to play mascot tonight but having little choice, I stood with a yawn. "Let me wash my face first."

Seth followed me to the bathroom and caged me in with one hand hanging from the top of the doorpost, the other on the side. "You were right about Bruce."

No duh. I squinted into the mirror. Bloodshot eyes surrounded by puffy bags. One thing for sure, I didn't need alcohol to look drunk. I rubbed the sleep from my eyes and flipped on the faucet. I needed a serious pick-me-up and doubted I'd find a cup of coffee any time soon. I held my hands under the chilled water and braced myself for a dash of cold. It had to be done.

Seth leaned against the doorjamb. "How did you know?"

"About what?" *On the count of three. One. Two—*

"Bruce."

My hands stilled under the near freezing stream. *Bruce and Seth sitting in a tree. How could I not know?* I smiled. "Seriously?"

One. Two. Three. I splashed my face and sucked in more air than needed along with a bit of water. Hacking a lung like the moron I was, I fumbled for the towel on the rack and raked it over my eyes.

Blinded by terry cloth and not expecting Seth to block my path, I ran straight into him. His hands slipped behind my back and caught me before I could fall. Just as quickly, he released me. My face to his chest, I was as close as I could get without touching. The heat from his body radiated like a furnace, while his fruity body wash teased my senses. Only my boy Seth could get away with that feminine fragrance and still be as hot as hell.

He brought his leg up and planted it on the other side of the frame. "Yeah. Seriously." His voice was as serious as the word.

As much as I wanted to resist, I couldn't help but meet his gaze. His piercing blue eyes penetrated me. No games. He wanted answers, and he wanted them now. Kinda sexy intimidating. *Meow*. My heart went thumpa thump thump.

"Don't be silly." I needed air—a cleansing breath not entangled with his scent. I pushed by and thanked God when Seth's leg fell easily. "You can't keep anything from me. I've known you since the first grade."

"Just remember. That goes two ways."

Does he know how I feel about him? Don't look. Don't look. He'll see it in your eyes. God, I hope my walk isn't stiff. It feels funky. Just play it cool. I threw the towel on the bed and grabbed a comb off the dresser.

Seth padded behind me. "Do you think anyone else knows?"

Really taking the time to think about his question, I worked through the snags in my hair. Did his occasional gaga eyes give him away? Someone would have said something by now, right? I didn't know what he did this afternoon, but I couldn't imagine receiving an invitation to the biggest jock frat house on campus if his secret was out. "Doubt it."

"It's not just Bruce; it's the Cheyenne thing too. I totally blew it."

What? I faced him. "I thought you didn't even like her."

"She's not that bad." My disbelief must have shown on my face because he immediately backtracked. "No. Not like that. It's just. I thought she'd be a safe bet. At least for a little while. You know? With her, there'd be no questioning looks. No questions asked."

"I could have been that for you, Seth." I wanted my voice to be strong... determined, but my words came out weak and shaky.

Seth's head cocked to the side as he considered me. Hope soared, and the corners of my mouth lightened. I pressed my lips flat, holding back the smile which wanted to break through.

"No, you couldn't." He shook his head. "It wouldn't work."

I blinked once. Twice. My almost smile wavered, and my chin trembled. Lord no. I was on the brink of a meltdown. The muscles in my neck clamped so tightly, it threatened to cave in. I turned my back to Seth and cleared my throat as I returned the comb to its proper place and slipped on my shoes. I stiffened at his footsteps.

He wrapped his arms around me, resting his chin on the top of my head. Sweet comfort. Warm, like a blanket and all encompassing. "It would be wrong. The things we'd have to do to convince everyone. It's hard enough pretending with someone like Cheyenne. You're my only friend. I don't want to ever lose that."

My heart broke, but I refused to cry. Damn it, I wouldn't. Even if I had to blink a thousand times.

Hope. It was such a small thing but hurt like hell when dashed. I wanted nothing more than for Seth to look at me the way he looked at Bruce. I would have taken pretend. That was better than nothing.

I swallowed the pain in my throat and pulled away. "Yeah. You're right. We better go."

The skin on the back of my neck prickled where I knew he stared, but I wouldn't give him the benefit of seeing my tears. No way. I avoided eye contact as I walked around him, grabbed my jacket, and opened the door wide. "After you."

Seth paused in front of me. I clamped my jaw tight and held my chin high, which put my eye level to his chest. Good enough. I didn't have to look him straight in the eye to show pride. I just needed to keep the tears from falling. *Walk away, Seth. Just walk away, damn it!*

His chest lifted and fell, sending a minty puff of air my way. "Walk or bike? It'll be nine o'clock by the time we get there regardless."

"Walk, I guess."

"Right." He left me holding the door as he headed down the hall. I closed my eyes and took a few calming breaths before I followed.

Chapter 4

♥

The walk to Bruce's frat house took about fifteen minutes. Yet I swore it dragged into the longest fifteen minutes of my life. Not a word passed through Seth's lips, and I wasn't about to break radio silence. Just as well. I didn't want to play like everything was super. The charade was hard enough as it was. One wrong word from my buddy, and it'd be the end of me. Just the idea of turning into a sniveling baby twisted my insides into a tight wad.

"This is it," Seth said as we approached the frat house. Bold Greek letters ran down the side—an announcement to the world this was Alpha Epsilon domain. Above the wide porch a banner read:

The Party Starts Here
Fall Rush Week
Pledge Alpha Epsilon

Seth's hand encircled my bicep before he pulled me flush to him, side to side. The heat of his body penetrated through my jacket. Usually the sensation was a wonderful reminder of his presence... an offer of warmth and security. Tonight, thoughts of how fleeting it would be bombarded me. Close contact now, but soon he'd adventure away and leave me behind as always. I'd play my role as nothing more than an extra in his cast.

"Ready?" Though the upturn of Seth's lips was slight, the excitement on his face reached all the way to his sparkling blue eyes. He wasn't even aware he'd crushed my soul with his off-handed rejection. Kudos for him.

As for me, I couldn't find the motivation to lift the corners of my mouth into a return smile. "Yeah. I guess."

"Here we go." Seth's hand slid into mine as he led me the last few feet to the porch. Before we made it halfway up the stairs, a couple of co-eds stumbled out the house laughing and jabbering. Like a bulldozer, one bumped invisible me hard enough to push me down a step.

"Excuse you," she yelled over her shoulder and kept going.

"Excuse me?" I stared at Seth. "Excuse *me*? What gives?"

He shrugged and dragged me the rest of the way up the stairs.

Dink blocked the entrance with his towering body and beamed a dimpled grin at me. "It's about time. I wasn't sure you were coming."

"It's still early." Seth ushered me forward with a gentle push on my shoulder blade.

Dink stepped back, making way like a door opening. If the blond Goliath had added creaking sound effects, he'd be the perfect stand in. "Bill and Bruce are over there playing information desk."

I followed his gaze to a far corner where a crowd gathered, the top of Bruce's dark hair peaking over the throng of people.

"Cool." Seth headed toward his one true love, pulling me along like a child.

"Actually…" Dink caught my arm, stretching me between the two guys like a tug-of-war rope. "Alex can come with me."

Seth's eyes narrowed as he focused on Dink before reconsidering me. Right then and there, I knew his exact thoughts: could he get away with abandoning me with Dink so he could sneak some alone time with Bruce?

I tried to keep my jaw relaxed despite the building resentment making me want to gnash my teeth like a junkyard dog. He had a lot of nerve dragging me out of bed only to ditch me the first chance he had and with some guy I barely knew. If he wanted to be like that, screw him! I'd make it easy for him. I disengaged my hand from Seth's. "I'll be fine."

Dink pulled me closer. "That's right. I'll make sure she stays out of trouble."

I snuck a peek at Dink in time to see him wink. *Trouble. Right.* I planned on giving Seth plenty of that when I got him alone again. Perhaps I wasn't the third wheel in a lineup next to Cheyenne, but Seth left no doubt in my mind, I was when it came to Bruce. *As if I asked to be here!*

"I'll meet up with you later, and we'll walk back together," Seth said as he backed off.

I resisted the urge to throw the bird as he turned away. With my mood dialing to cranky bitch, I was grateful for the distraction Dink provided.

"Thirsty?" he asked.

"I guess." I didn't even bother looking at him. It just wasn't worth the effort to crane my neck.

Dink guided me through the house, sometimes even putting a hand out as if pushing through a tackle. Cute that he couldn't leave the game on the field. No doubt he'd tuck me under his arm like a football if he could get away with it. Watching Dink move amused me enough to cool me down from Seth's brush-off.

The beginning of a smile found its way to my lips.

"Well?" Dink crouched in front of one of the five coolers surrounding a refreshment table. "Only thing about Rush, guidelines say it has to be dry."

"Dry? As in no pool parties?"

He laughed—a good hardy one lacking in mockery. "No alcohol. Dry means no alcohol."

That got my full smile. It was hard to hold on to my frustrations while stuck with someone as good-natured as Dink.

"Still plenty of fun to be had though." He did his wink-wink thing and opened the cooler stuffed with cans, bottles, and melting ice pooling in water. "What'll it be?"

I looked inside but couldn't make out any brands. "Cola?"

"Sure." Dink dug deep, and I cringed at the thought of the freezing water making contact with skin. The arctic plunge had to be killer, but he kept at it until he pulled out a red can. He shook the droplets off his hand and grabbed a napkin from the table, grinning as he wiped the can free of moisture. "Cold."

"I bet."

"Want a cup?"

"No. This is fine."

Dink cracked my cola open with a fizz and passed the soda to me. "Come on."

I took one sip before Dink grabbed my arm with his icy palm and whisked me through the crowd faster than I could say, "uh."

He stopped in front of green curtains and smiled so big his face had to hurt. "Alpha Epsilon!"

Throughout the house, others echoed his shout.

"Show time." He parted the drapes and pulled me behind them.

My warning bells went off like a fire drill as I found myself in a dark enclosed space with the giant of a man. I couldn't help but be nervous. *Never show fear.* I giggled like a dizzy twit to cover my unease. "I hope this isn't the kissing booth."

Dink chuckled. "It could be..." His voice deepened, which seemed impossible considering its already low timber. "If you want."

"Certainly not what I'd expected." I reached for the curtain, but he stayed my hand.

"Wait." He opened a door I'd missed upon first arriving. "I was kidding. Ladies first."

Okay, obviously the guy had flipped his lid if he expected me to descend into the dark unknown. "I don't think so."

He turned on the lights leading downstairs to a basement. "We've been planning this party for months. You're just in time for the highlights."

I hesitated as my parents' wisdom from days long ago nagged me. Going strange places with virtual strangers was a no-no. Heck, Seth's little sister would say to turn away from the dungeon of doom.

"Well?" Dink still held my hand but made no physical move to urge me forward.

Quit being silly, I told myself. Seth knew whom I was with. Dink would be crazy to pull anything funny knowing he'd be the first people would look for if I showed up missing. Besides, I didn't get any bad vibes from him.

I started down the steps. "How about you go first and be my cushion in case I fall?"

Only a slight hint of a smile remained on his lips, but it was warm. "It'd be my pleasure."

He took the narrow staircase sideways while I followed. Though I joked about him being my safety net, I was glad he went first. The stairs were so steep visions of tripping haunted me all the way down, and it certainly didn't help the last quarter lacked rails.

Dink reached the bottom and turned back with his hand outstretched. I grabbed him, not trusting my shaking legs to keep me from stumbling. His meaty paw was engulfing as his sausage fingers wrapped around my wrists.

Breakable. That was the word which came to me while alone in the bulk of his presence. Though more vulnerable than ever, his gentleness gave me a sense of safety as I took the remaining steps with his help.

His hand lingered a moment longer than necessary before sliding down to the small of my back. "This way."

A little push was all it took to guide me in the direction he wanted. For many the gesture might mean little. For me, it was more, sending a tingle of specialness coursing through my body. Surely this was the way celebrities felt—important enough someone cared they reached their destination safely.

He led me to a fuse box and opened the case. His eyes grew wide with a crazy gleam, his grin all teeth. At any moment he could burst out laughing. He spread his fingers across four switches marked with tiny white x's and flicked them.

Though the basement stayed illuminated, the entry to the main house went dark.

A shriek from upstairs.

"What just happened?" a girl cried out. Then everyone was talking at once.

"Calm down," some guy said. "Calm down, already!"

The crowd simpered to a dull roar.

"I'll check it out. Nobody move." I recognized the voice as Bruce.

Dink snickered beside me, his shoulders shaking as he worked unsuccessfully to stifle outright laughter. With his eyes glued to his wristwatch and free hand hovering over breaker switches marked with red dots, he was a man on a mission.

"What are you doing?" I asked.

Dink's eyes flickered to me before returning to his watch. "One sec. It's almost time. Five. Four. Three. Two." He flipped the breakers.

Upstairs, the people gasped loud enough to suck most of the air out of a room, but from my position in the basement, I only saw a faint glow. "I don't think all the lights came on."

"Just wait."

With everyone upstairs talking at once, the commotion had turned thunderous.

I glanced back. He smiled so big, the dimple in his cheek looked like a never-ending hole.

"Welcome to Alpha Epsilon," a male shouted from upstairs, though I couldn't place the voice. "Let the games begin!"

Smoke rolled down the steps.

"Oh my god! Fire!" I took a step back, bumping into Dink. Trapped in the basement with nowhere to run I couldn't decide which would be worse: suffocating on the smoke fumes or becoming a crispy critter.

Dink chuckled, and his midsection vibrated against my back. "Come on. Check it out."

I dug in my heels as he used his bulk to push me forward and "help" me up the stairs.

Run away from the light, the trickster in my head yelled. My feet disappeared into the cloud of smoke rolling down the steps. Only Dink at my back kept me moving.

I continued, expecting at any moment to come face to face with the blazing heat of a fire. Yet the air felt amazingly cool. I reached the top, pulled back the curtain, and froze.

A dance club greeted me. Black lights put an eerie glow on everyone and made shirts luminescent while giant hoses lay strategically around the room, expelling white fog.

Standing on a table, Bruce raised his cup high, sloshing liquid over the side. "Alpha Epsilon."

The crowd returned his shout, me included.

"Listen up," Bruce said. "We have several events, so don't all congregate to one place." He pointed to the stairs, hallways, and doors as he rattled off each station.

Laughing, I turned to Dink. "This is awesome. How did you do it?"

"Dry ice," was his simple response.

Students headed in different directions, giving wide berth to a shark fin weaving through the crowd.

"And that?"

Dink wagged his brows. "One of the early pledges sliding on a skateboard."

I laughed until my stomach clenched tight enough to double me over. "Ow, ow, ow."

"You okay?" Dink's hand landed on my back, rubbing gentle circles.

I forced myself to relax, and my stomach muscles uncoiled. "A cramp."

"Want to be a pirate?"

"Aye, aye, captain!" I said as I straightened.

Chapter 5

♥

By the time we returned to the first floor, the fog had dispersed to a pathetically thin layer. I didn't care. Still high from walking the plank, I searched for my next big adventure. I grabbed Dink's arm, bouncing a little in my excitement. "Now what?"

Dink's teeth glowed in the black light as he grinned, surveying the room. His smile froze, transformed into a grimace. Odd how similar the two expressions were.

"Get off me!" Bruce said from behind.

I turned just in time to see Seth fall and flop around like a fish out of water.

Bruce took a step forward with his face set in a scowl. Towering over my friend, he pulled his boot back and let it loose.

Seth lifted off the floor with a grunt and curled over like a dead ant.

My life with my BFF flashed before my eyes: peeling dried glue from our hands in second grade, him begging me for a turn as I became Darth Raven in the Knights of the Old Republic, signing his cast after he failed to catch a fly ball and it cracked his arm, searching for our caps after we'd thrown them at graduation.

A scream tore my throat raw as I rushed the football jock.

Bruce turned in slow motion.

A bazillion miles separated me from him, giving him plenty of time to transform his scrunched angry face into one of surprise. Not until both my feet pushed from the ground, sending me airborne did I realize I'd lost my mind. My shrieking ended in a squawk as five-one, one hundred pound me took on gigantic buffalo man. Bruce caught me with open arms, and my nose bashed into his pectoral. Instant tears filled my eyes as I slid down his chest like melting wax. The only thing which kept me from falling at his feet was his hand wrapped tight around one arm like I was a naughty child.

"What the fuck do you think you're doing?" He shook me, and his thumb bit into my armpit. It hurt like hell but also tickled. My uncontrolled laughter bubbled over as I fought to pry his fingers from my tickle spot.

"Hey. Let her go." Dink had finally caught up to save the day.

Bruce tossed me like a rag doll, and I stumbled before bouncing off Dink. Putting his athletic reflexes to good use, he wrapped an arm around my waist, keeping me standing.

Seth moaned.

I circled Bruce, wishing I had the strength to shove him out of the way, and dropped to my knees to brush my friend's bangs out of his eyes. "Oh god, Seth. Are you okay?"

His dark eyes focused on me, or at least they tried as they swirled sporadically. Something was off about them, but I couldn't pinpoint it. Then I did a double take. Seth's eyes were so dark, he looked demonic. I leaned closer. Pupils dilated, the light blue rings of his irises were nearly non-existent.

"Oh my god!" I twisted around, frowning so hard at Bruce the start of a headache formed. "What did you do to him?"

Bruce blinked then his teeth pulled back. "I didn't do anything. The fuckin' pervert came on to me."

"You're lying!" I returned my attention to Seth, putting Bruce's ridiculous words out of my head. I knew my boy. He was so deep in the closet he couldn't find his way out with a map and compass. I set his head in my lap and ran my fingers through his hair checking for bumps. "He'd never do anything like that."

"Fuck you."

"Watch it, man." The warning in Dink's voice caught me by surprise, but I appreciated he'd come to my defense.

I found nothing off with Seth's head and gave his cheek a few light slaps. "Seth? Seth? I think we need to get you to the hospital."

A moan was his only response, and that worried me more than anything.

"Let me help." Dink knelt beside me. My friend was nothing more than dead weight, as Dink set him upright and surveyed the gathering crowd. "Bill, let's get him on his feet."

Seth's darts partner cast a good long look toward Bruce who didn't even bother to acknowledge him.

I couldn't believe it. My friend needed help, and the idiot was looking for permission from the guy who'd beaten my friend senseless? That was bullshit.

"Forget it." I stood and dug in my pocket for my cell. "I'm calling 911."

"Fine," Bruce said between clenched teeth. "Help her."

Bill and Dink each grabbed one of Seth's biceps and lifted.

"Whoa." Seth gave a lazy smile. Maybe he wasn't injured after all. Alcohol came to mind, but Dink had said this was a dry party. Drugs maybe? Seth's head lolled to the side as he stared at Bruce. "God, you're hot."

The crowd gasped as one, me included, and Bruce took a step forward with a raised fist.

Dink's hand landed on Bruce's chest, keeping the guy at a distance. "Let it go."

Bruce's face transformed into something too ugly for words as he jabbed his finger at my friend. "If you ever touch me again, I swear I'll kill you."

Seth giggled.

For a moment, time stood still. It was as if everyone was in awe and couldn't formulate their next action. At least, that was how I felt.

Bruce put life back in motion with a disgusted shake of the head. "Get him the hell out of here." He pushed through the crowd and disappeared upstairs.

"Jerk," I mumbled.

"I knew there was something off about him," some bimbo said. The voice gave way to a face as Cheyenne stepped to the forefront, giving me a satisfied smirk. "Yep. I should have known that night at Johnson Hall."

She made eye contact with a few in the crowd. What did she expect? Their affirmation? She nodded. Talk about the woman scorned. "Yep I knew it. You heard him, right? He'd have been all over—"

"Will you *shut* up?" I stepped up to the plate though I barely reached her chin. "You're too shallow to have your own opinion."

"Back off." Cheyenne's face bore down on me until her nose almost touched mine.

I hated the way the air from her nostrils tickled my upper lip. Oh how I hoped she touched me. Sure my friend was gay, but no way I'd let someone make him out to be some kind of horny bandit, preying on unsuspecting frat boys. Rage bubbled in me, and my balled fists itched for an outlet. "If—"

"Alex. Do you really have time for this?" Dink snapped me back to reality, putting a damper on my need to beat Cheyenne into submission.

I wanted to back down. Truly I did, but fear prevented me. Bullies always looked for weaknesses, and Cheyenne was no different. If I let things go, she wouldn't stop at trying to turn people against Seth. Next time she'd try to incite a gay bashing. I uncurled my fingers but refused to look away. Her dull green eyes versus mine. Except my right one suddenly developed a tingle. *Crap!*

Cheyenne blinked, and uncertainty played in her eyes.

Right on.

"Alex?" Dink called.

Cheerleader bimbo straightened. "You're not worth the effort."

"Riiiiight." I mentally chalked my finger down the scoreboard and suppressed the smile pulling the corners of my mouth.

"Alex?" Sharpness had found its way into Dink's deep voice. "What should we do with him?"

My eyes travel to my friend dangling between the two bulky football players, but my mind came up with nothing. I silently pled with those surrounding us, hoping for an answer. What I got were the blank stares of curious bystanders more interested in a drama then offering assistance.

"You got a car?" Dink asked.

"No." My hope of getting Seth to the hospital, much less anywhere else faded, and 911 popped into my head again.

"We'll use mine." Dink didn't even wait for a response. With the help of Bill, he dragged Seth out the door. The only choice left for me was how close I should follow.

Chapter 6

♥

The bright lights reflecting off shiny surfaces did nothing to alleviate the dour atmosphere of the hospital. Worse, the heavy scent of disinfectants assaulted my nose yet failed to mask the lingering sickness in the air. Meanwhile, the gatekeeper before me with her bored expression and tired sighs did nothing to lighten the situation.

I leaned against the counter and tried my umpteeth tactic at getting information about Seth. "I'm the one who brought him in."

"Patient information is only available on a need to know basis per the Privacy Act." What was she? Some kind of automaton? That was the third time the receptionist had fed me that stupid line. And 'per the Privacy Act?' Who in the world said 'per' anything?

Out of arguments, I stared at her and wished I had mind manipulation powers. "Forget it."

The receptionist faked a pleasant smile which bordered on patronizing. "Sorry I couldn't be more helpful. HIPAA laws."

"Yeah right. Freakin' blows."

Ms. Stuffy-Pants raised a single eyebrow before proceeding to clack away at her keyboard.

Yeah. Screw you too, lady. I pushed off the receptionist counter and returned to the waiting area.

"Well?" Dink stood as I approached. Considering his size, I wished he'd have stayed seated.

"Nothing." I walked past and sprawled in a hard plastic chair, dangling my arms over the rests to keep from slipping further. "If you want to leave, I'm fine. I don't know when I'll get to see him."

Dink sat next to me, and his thick thighs brushed against mine. "I'll wait it out with you. You'll need a ride home."

"No biggie." I sat straighter—my discrete attempt to pull away from his leg which doused me with uncomfortable but not at all unpleasant heat. "I'll take the bus."

"No, you won't." He leaned back and crossed his legs at the ankle. Matter settled. Case closed.

"Thank you."

Time stretched between us in silence. Not that I minded the quiet; Dink's presence was enough. I didn't have the courage to express how much his company meant to me. The only other person who'd stick with me through a haul like this was Seth, and Seth was the reason I was here. Still, I couldn't help but look the gift horse in the mouth. "Why are you doing this?"

A shy smile lit his face, dimpling his right cheek. "Seriously?"

"Well yeah. Bill left before you could even get Seth in the car. After what Bruce and Cheyenne said, aren't you afraid of what others will think?"

His smile turned upside down, and his entire demeanor darkened. "And what would that be?"

I looked away. I couldn't bear to say it. Admitting people might turn away from my friend because he was gay seemed like a betrayal. "Forget it."

"What? That I'm gay?"

I tensed. *Exactly.* "No. That's not what I said."

"But it was what you meant."

"Maybe."

The edge in his voice softened. "I'm only interested in one opinion right now."

"Yeah? Whose would that be? Bill? Bruce?"

He laughed low. "No."

"Never mind. It's none of my business." I scooted forward until only half my butt remained on the chair, ready for takeoff. It was all I could do to remain seated and not return to the reception desk, demanding answers.

"I wouldn't be here if I didn't care." Dink's hand splayed across my back, and a warning light shot off like a blown transformer.

I turned slowly, afraid of what I'd find.

His intense gaze burned into me, trapped me, searched. Surely this giant of a man who dwarfed me couldn't want to hookup. Yet his questioning green eyes said plenty. He had the hots for me. All the signs fell into place. The special attention at Johnson Hall. The invitation to the frat party. Whisking me to the basement. This? *Holy crap! He had the hots for me!*

Dink. Attractive? Sure. I'd be a fool to think otherwise with the orange starbursts of his eyes captivating me like kaleidoscopes. Not to mention the dimple in his right cheek creating an invisible sign over his head which flashed ADORABLE. Of course, he was cute. No denying that one.

I entertained the idea of dating him. My heart even sped up a bit, sending heat straight to my face. Oh yeah, I entertained the thought... all for about two seconds. One scene ended the short daydream: walking hand-in-hand next to the colossus. The size difference between the two of us was astronomical and put a damper on the whole fantasy. I supposed being with Dink would be okay if we never stood, never went anywhere, just sat in these seats for eternity.

Fleshy warmth landed on my leg, jolting me from my deep thoughts. I zeroed in on Dink's hand caressing my knee. He was all around me, creating a jumble of feelings. I wanted to bolt from the unfamiliar intimacy, while the desire to nestle in the safety of his protective enclosure grew strong. My head became airy like a balloon on the verge of floating away.

I remembered to breathe, but there wasn't enough air between us. Swept in the dizziness of it all, my eyes played tricks on me. Dink seemed closer than he'd been only a millisecond ago. No illusion. He *was* leaning toward me. Closer. Closer. His eyes focused on my mouth, making me self-conscious. I licked my lips, and he paused, his pupils dilating in the bright light.

My heart went into a panicked convulsion. *Oh lord. He's going to kiss me.*

The soft fleshiness of his mouth brushed against mine, and a tingling started in my stomach. Was this what they meant by butterflies? His tongue skimmed my bottom lip.

"Alex Carmichael."

I jumped to my feet at my name over the intercom.

"Please come to the front desk. Alex Carmichael, please come to the front desk." A slight clatter and the mike went dead.

"That's me!" My lungs worked overtime as if I'd run a marathon.

"Want me to go with you?" The sparkle in Dink's eyes overshadowed the serious set of his lips.

"No. No. I'll go." I raced away.

I ran my tongue over the kiss which lingered on my lips and savored the soda sweetness which wasn't there before. A real kiss. As Seth's invisible sidekick, I'd never experienced one before. It was like a triple shot of espresso, but unlike the bitter drink I hated, I wanted more.

The receptionist pasted on a mechanical smile as I approached. "May I help you?"

"I'm Alex Carmichael."

"Wonderful." Deadpan voice fit well with her stale personality. She rested a clipboard on the counter and placed a pen on top. "Please sign in here. Room 179. Patient name: Seth Richards. I'll need a picture ID."

I passed her my license and wasted no time scribbling in the information. "I have to get my friend."

"Sorry." She took the sign in sheet and returned my license. "You're the only one authorized to go back."

"But—" One look at her parting mouth ready for a rebuttal, and I gave up the fight. "Never mind. I'll tell him."

"Of course. Let me know when you're ready." Her eyes focused on the monitor, her fingers tapping the keyboard as if I'd never been there.

I returned to Dink, feeling more protected than dwarfed when he stood this time. I couldn't meet his eyes. My lips remembered the kiss, and they throbbed in anticipation for another. Just the thought sent heat creeping up my neck and beyond until I was sure even my hair follicles sweated. I took a deep breath. "They're going to let me see Seth."

"Great." Dink reached for his jacket.

I touched his arm but jerked away as the uncertainty of the situation and my feelings hit me. "You can't go," I blurted. "They'll only let me."

"That makes sense." He tossed his coat back on the seat.

I felt as if I owed him something more. An explanation. An excuse. Anything. Instead, I stood in awkward silence, waiting for him to say it was okay to leave. I glanced at the double doors barring me from my best friend before returning my attention to Dink.

His eyes flickered back and forth over my face as if trying to settle on one feature. What did he see? I felt like an open book, exposed under his scrutiny. Too much, too soon. *I don't know you. I'm in love with my best friend, and you're confusing me.*

"Are you hungry? We can check if the cafeteria is open when you come back." Dink's dimple made an appearance again. "It's not like a real date, but given the circumstances..."

My head nodded as if there was only one answer, not bothering to ask if I was along for the ride.

"Great. I'll wait for you right here." He sat with his legs spread wide, arms resting on his thighs. He seemed so sure, completely confident, while I was a twisted mess of emotional muddiness.

I plodded to the front desk like the zombie a single kiss from Dink had turned me into. My prior experience as wall decoration had not prepared me for the intensity, the turmoil of feelings which went with what I will forever remember as *my first kiss*.

Then guilt slammed me. Life was Seth and I. There'd been nothing before *US*. Even the occasional "girlfriend" along for the ride never came between me and my bud—the dynamic duo. Somehow the dynamic trio didn't quite sound right. Ménage à trois, anyone? No. Didn't think so.

The receptionist rolled bored eyes my way. "Ready?"

"Yeah."

She walked around the desk and led me to the double doors. One swipe of her card and the door spread open like a scene from Willy Wonka and the

Chocolate Factory. "Follow the blue line on the floor until you get to the nurses desk."

I stared at the lines under my feet: red, yellow, blue, and green. Each led down the corridor but split in different directions. This was it. In a few moments, I'd know what had gotten into Seth at the party. I stepped forward, wondering how the turn in events would affect my future... and Seth's—my friend who'd inadvertently came out of the closet tonight.

The doors behind me closed with finality. Without a doubt, I knew nothing would ever be the same.

Chapter 7

♥

I'm in love with my best friend. I followed the blue line repeating the phrase in my head despite the constant bombardment of Dink's lips against mine invading my thoughts. The quick pecks Seth and I exchanged from time to time meant nothing more than a friendly hello or goodbye... like a chaste hug between family members.

I longed for something more, prayed I would be the exception for Seth. That he'd realized his love for me surpassed any attraction he might have for guys. False hope, sure, but I held fast to the dream. To do otherwise would be like the outfielders giving up the chase as realization hit: the ball was flying out of the park.

Seth wasn't out of reach, not yet. He was my best friend and knew me better than anyone, accepted my anti-social ways, didn't question my sunbathing despite not needing a tan...

Your quirks are what make you, you, Alex, he'd said. *If I wanted to hang with someone with a different personality, don't you think I would have done so already?*

We had a connection I could never imagine with Dink, regardless of the bit of tongue action which had short circuited my neurons.

Why couldn't Seth kiss me like that? I slowed to a stop. The last conversation I'd had with him hit me full force. The magnitude of the realization knocked me back, forced me to use the wall as support. I had absolutely no chance with Seth. None. Reality weighed on me until even my eyelids grew too heavy to keep open.

Seth had already turned me down flat—deemed me unworthy of the charade he played with other girls. At least I would have been in on the masquerade and not blown his cover. I would have been the safe bet, but he didn't even want that.

"Do you need help?"

My eyes popped open to a wall of flowers... gobs of colorful flowers against a blue background. Nurses' outfits were nothing like the plain whites portrayed on TV. Sitting in the waiting room, teddy bear, balloon, and polka dot prints galore had passed through the doors. Add Nurse Fran's—RN, BSN, so the name tag said—scrubs to the mix and the hospital could put on a fashion show.

She leaned closer, concern masking her face as she touched my shoulder. "Are you okay?"

"Yeah." I pushed off the wall and tried to make normal. "Just fortifying myself before visiting a friend. It's been a long night."

She gave a kind smile. After dealing with Ms. Fake Personality in the front, I'd given up on common courtesy in this place. Nurse Fran was a welcomed relief. "Know where you're going?"

"Follow the blue line to the nurses' desk."

"Sounds like you're heading to my ward. Turn the corner and ring the bell if no one's at the station."

"Thanks." I smiled and hoped it looked as genuine as hers. In truth, I wasn't feeling it. Not with so many complications in my life. "I better get going. He's probably waiting for me."

Fran stepped back, and I continued on my way—head up, shoulders back without an ounce of the strength I tried to fake.

Around the corner, I approached a deserted nurses' station and tapped the metal bell, sending a soft tingle into the air. With the area void of carpet and full of hard surfaces, the acoustics were fantastic, and the echoes bounced off the walls in a fading symphony.

"One moment." A heavyset woman waddled out of a room. She had the type of features people would say, *she has such a pretty face. It's too bad she's so big.*

Long auburn hair cascaded over her shoulders, rich brown irises—some would call them doe eyes, a cute little pert nose, symmetrical features perfectly proportioned. Then there was the elephant in the room. The issue most people were too polite to mention in her presence.

She situated herself behind the nurses' station, and the chair squealed as she plunked down with a heavy sigh. A smile formed on her lips, bringing a sparkle to her eyes full of genuine joy. "Now. What can I do for you?"

Some smiles existed which a person couldn't help but return. The woman before me had one of those, and the warmth of it stole away my worries.

"My name is Alex Carmichael. I was sent from the front desk. My friend, Seth Richards? He's here."

"Ah. Mr. Richards. I'm Bianca, his nurse." She chuckled. "Quite a charmer, that one. He's been asking about you." She leaned forward, squashing the papers on the desk with her ample chest, and pointed to one of the open doors. "One seventy-nine. Knock before you enter."

With so much security getting into the fortress, her willingness to let me wander into patient rooms alone took me off guard. I hesitated.

"Go on, dear." She clasped her fingers together and rested her chin on top, eluding peacefulness, as if she was comfortable in her skin whereas others were not.

"Thanks." I walked the short distance to Seth's room and paused.

The room lacked privacy with only a white curtain separating the occupants from passing people. Like the charade masking Seth's secret, the flimsy material offered a weak veil to the happenings on the other side.

The little comfort I'd gained from Bianca dissipated like away team fans after a losing game. Despite her comment that my friend was a charmer, Seth was all show. He had to be devastated.

I took a deep breath and knocked. "Seth. It's me. May I come in?"

"Late much? Get in here," the invisible voice of Seth called.

I stepped inside and pulled back the curtain.

An elderly black man with a thick afro stared at me with a Kool-Aid smile. "Wrong one, hun."

"Ding dong. Over here," Seth said from further in the room.

"Sorry." I zipped the curtain shut and rushed along.

Seth lounged on the hospital bed with an IV dangling from his hand. I rubbed the back of mine wondering if he'd been out of it when they stuck him.

Seth's side of the room was claustrophobic with the curtain blocking the entrance. Despite having the window side, no one had bothered to open the blinds. I did the deed and met darkness marked with a few square lights. Where were the neon signs?

"We got the view facing the inner courtyard. Great, right?" His voice lacked the enthusiasm of his words but mimicked my thoughts exactly. "At least I don't have to be here long. I check out in the morning. By nine o'clock, they said."

I faced him, unsure of where to begin. So I didn't.

"Can you get me some water?" He thrust a plastic jug my way.

I crossed my arms. "Are your legs broken?"

"Honestly? Still a bit wobbly." Truth be told, he didn't look all that great. His beach boy tan did nothing to hide the unhealthy pallor lurking underneath, while the light blue of the hospital gown only emphasized his bloodshot eyes.

Just like that, I fell into the role of personal assistant and took the jug from his outstretched arms. "Where do I fill it?"

He shrugged. I rolled my eyes and went in search for Bianca.

She saw me coming and rose to her feet with an effort which made me feel guilty for bothering her. "I'll take that."

I tried not to cringe as she hobbled around the desk. "If you show me where—"

"No. I'd have you get it yourself, but the ice maker is behind a locked door. I need to make another round anyway." She took the jug with a smile and shooed me. "Go ahead and visit. I'll bring this to Mr. Richards' room."

Mr. Richards. The first time she'd called him that, I'd thought she was joking. To hear the formality again sort of freaked me out. I expected Seth's father to come strolling around the corner at any moment.

My friend had a queasy half-smile on his face when I returned, but that didn't stop me from getting around to the question on my mind. "Will you tell me what happened already?"

Seth's head fell against the pillow like his neck had the muscle tone of a noodle, and his eyes slid shut. "Someone slipped me a roofie."

For someone who'd been drugged, my boy sure was casual about it.

I didn't buy the calm facade. Seth could pull the acting game with the rest of the world but not with me. I'd known the real him far too long to be fooled. "Who would do that?"

"How should I know?"

"Well, you're the one who drank it. I'd think you'd know who spiked your drink."

"Look." His eyes popped wide open, and we locked in a stare down. "I remember being in your dorm. I remember halfway walking to the party. I remember being in a car. And I remember waking up here. That's all. Now could you leave me alone about it!?"

"Snarky drama queen doesn't suit you."

"Will you let it go already?"

"Yeah. But first, just one question."

"Fine." He rolled his eyes and dropped his head again in feigned sleep.

"Are you going to tell your parents?"

"It's not like I can keep it a secret once they get the bill."

"Not thaaaat." I stretched out the 'a' and crossed the 't' with a sharp tick of my tongue. "I mean about being gay."

The man behind the curtain gave a cough, reminding me we weren't alone.

Seth sat ramrod straight. "Shit, Alex. What the hell is wrong with you?" He looked at the curtain like he had x-ray vision which he could use to wipe his neighbor's memory.

"I didn't think it was much of a secret, considering..."

He put on his Mr. Squinty-eyed mask while his upper lip twitched on one side. "Considering what?"

"Considering the way you came on to Bruce."

"What!" His eyes flickered like he had sand stuck in them, and then it hit me. The roofie had blasted his memory to shreds.

"Here we go." Bianca walked in carrying Seth's water jug and placed it on the end table near his bed. "Now just because I brought you a drink doesn't mean you can go crazy on the call button like you did earlier. This isn't the Hilton."

She patted Seth on his foot before moving on. "How ya doing, Mr. Gray? Are you decent?"

"Enough for you," The man behind the curtains said.

No privacy, I stared at Seth in abject silence trying to decipher his unreadable expression while Nurse Bianca did whatever she did to make the other patient grunt and moan. With a weary sigh, the noises stopped.

"I'll give you a bit more time with your friend then I'll come back and check your vitals, Mr. Richards," Bianca called from the doorway. Her heavy steps faded down the hall.

If only I could follow her to anywhere but here. Any place which didn't involve being ground zero in this ugly, confusing mess of a situation titled *Seth the Closet Gay Comes Out*. No escaping, I bit the bullet. "I only know what Bruce said and what I saw."

Seth's eyes narrowed. "And that was?"

"You on the floor, Bruce on the verge of beating you into next week, him saying you came on to him, and..." The connectors from my brain to my mouth snapped closed, putting my rambling to a halt.

Seth tensed so much, the muscles in his neck rolled into cords, and the blankets bunched in his fists. "And what?"

"And..." I swallowed, fearing Seth for the first time. He was so tightly coiled I expected him to jump out of bed and strangle me at any moment.

"Tell me!"

"You said he was hot," I blurted.

Seth closed his eyes and took a deep breath before exhaling. For a moment, he looked peaceful. If I'd not been in here the whole time, I'd have sworn he'd just had the best massage of his life. Then his eyes flicked open. The angry red in them made them perfect for the before picture in a Visine commercial. "Get out."

His voice was so low, I wasn't sure I'd heard him right. All I knew was I hadn't seen Seth this close to tears in years.

"Get out." He winced as he reached behind him, but that didn't stop the pillow which came flying at me on his upswing and hitting me in the face before falling to the floor. "I said, GET OUT!"

I backed away and tangled in the curtain. On the verge of panic, I fought the fabric with my fists until they released me and allowed me to escape into the hall.

Bianca lumbered toward me. Her body swayed with each step, giving a fluent effect similar to the waves of the ocean. She paused at the door. "What's going on?"

"I told him with happened at the party," I said between ragged breaths.

The *yeah right* look she gave said I wasn't fooling her. Half-truths were better than nothing. If she wanted more, she could pump Seth for information. "You better leave now."

She didn't have to tell me twice. I stumbled over my shoes as I turned to leave and didn't look back. Lost in a world of unfamiliar loneliness, the blue line was my only guide. I wandered in a daze as tunnel vision turned my peripheral dim and fuzzy despite the bright hospital lights.

Seth had done more than kick me out of the room; he'd kicked me out of his life... abandoned me, and left a big gaping hole in my heart—the place I'd reserved only for him. Without my BFF, I only wanted to return to my dorm and forget the day ever happened.

Life refused me even that consolation. Seth needed me when the hospital released him in a few hours. Of course I'd wait for him. That was me—always on standby. The lackey.

I gave a mirthless laugh as I trudged through the corridors.

It wasn't right! I debated storming back to Seth and ripping him a new one. He acted like it was my fault he'd landed in the hospital.

I hadn't drugged him. I certainly wasn't the one who'd brushed him off to a virtual stranger. If anything, I'd stopped Bruce from turning him into a glob of broken bones. Yet my so-called friend treated me like I was the bad guy.

Screw that. I should just leave his ass, let him find his own ride. After the way he'd kicked me out, he deserved nothing less.

I slapped my hands against the double doors leading to the waiting room and pushed. The mechanical doors hardly budged. Oh how I hated them.

The barricade fueled my anger as I shook the metal bar. My braid took up the rhythm, bouncing between my shoulder blades. Pointless and ridiculous, the rational part of my brain said, but the release felt so good. At any moment I expected a security camera to pick up my moronic behavior. Images of psychiatrists with their straightjackets and needles pounding toward me slapped me back to sanity.

I froze with my hands clenched around the metal. My breaths came in harsh pants, while my heart tapped an irregular staccato.

Through the rectangular glass pane on the side of the door, Dink slept with his chin resting on his chest, legs crossed at the ankle, and arms akimbo. Asleep and from a distance, he wasn't nearly as imposing. Not exactly soft and cuddly, but for the first time I understood the meaning behind the phrase "nothing but a big teddy bear." But looks were as reliable as a screw ball—like Seth and his straight act.

Using the side of my fist, I mashed the button with the blue wheelchair, and the double doors parted. This was it. The minute I cleared the threshold, I'd be shut out, finalizing the chasm Seth set between us. As livid as I was, I couldn't bring myself to take the next step.

"Miss?" An unfamiliar woman leaned over the front counter, the previous receptionist nowhere in sight. "I'm going to have to ask that you not block the doors."

Too late for me to turn back, she'd made the choice for me. I forced one foot in front of the other, and the doors swished shut: me on one side, Seth on the other.

I was a marionette, and a puppet master controlled me. That was the only explanation, because

I don't recall walking to Dink yet somehow found myself in front of him.

His eyes cracked opened, and he drew his legs in. "How did it go?"

"What?" I asked before his words registered.

"Seth okay?"

Mentally? No. Physically? "I think so. Someone spiked his drink."

"Figures." Dink stood, making me David to his Goliath. "Food or dorms?"

"They'll release him in a few hours. Food, I guess."

"Great. I'm starved." Dink's hand landed on my back. His palm was warm, and my body heated beneath as if he was a hotplate. He guided me down a hall to the left, one step to my three.

"How do you know where to go?"

Dink smiled, highlighting that one deep dimple. "Red line. I asked at the desk."

Sure enough, the red line took us on a short walk to the cafeteria where I filled my tray with fare not so different from campus food and headed to the cashier.

"I got that." Dink scooted his tray next to mine and pulled his wallet from his back pocket. Money exchanged hands, and I followed him to a table.

Dink hunched over his meal, arms on either side like he was protecting his grub from prisoners.

"Thanks." I bit into an apple.

Dink popped a French fry in his mouth, but eating didn't stop him from talking. "For what?"

"For this." I waved my hand, taking in our late-night snack. "And for helping me with Seth."

He looked up, and his eyes searched mine. "What's with your friend anyway?"

Great. Here we go. I pulled a Twix commercial and took another bite of my apple.

Dink bowed his head and went back to work on his fries—one after another, sometimes in bundles as he shoved them in his mouth. "I shouldn't have asked." Another fry disappeared into the cavern named Dink.

My apple turned into a pile of tasteless mush on my tongue. I swallowed. "No. I guess the secret's out now." I stared at the top of his strawberry blond hair, wishing I could see his eyes. "Seth is gay."

Dink grabbed his cheeseburger and dipped it in ketchup. A quarter of it vanished in a single bite before he lifted an eyebrow at me, one cheek bulging to the size of a golf ball while he chewed.

Even though I couldn't read his expression, I still wanted to evaporate under the scrutiny.

He set his burger down, grabbed a napkin, and swiped his mouth. Leaning back in the booth with the napkin crushed in his fist, he finished chewing. His Adam's apple dipped a few times before he ran his tongue over his teeth with a slurping snap. "Thought so."

Thought so?

He tossed his napkin and grabbed his burger. "I suspected something was off with him by the way he was with Bruce the night we played darts."

"Off with him?" If Dink weren't my ride, I'd have left. There was nothing off about my friend. Sure, he was gay, but so what?

"Yeah." Dink hunched over his burger and devoured another quarter.

"What's that supposed to mean?"

His eyes never left me as he took his time finishing, the dimple in his cheek flashing as he chewed. I could have been a boring television program with the lack of emotion on his face. He swallowed the last bite and did the tongue over teeth smacking thing again. "Look." He brushed his bangs to the side. "I'm not saying anything's wrong with him. I'm just saying the signs were there. I'd like to say I was surprised, but who are we kidding?"

My eyes narrowed as I tried to determine if he had an issue with my friend. I got nothing. "Well?"

"Well what?" He grabbed his soda and downed half in three gulps.

"You got a problem with Seth being gay?"

Dink laughed as if I'd just told the greatest joke. "What do I care? He's Bruce's problem. It's not like he's into me or anything, right?" His brows drew down in stark slashes. "Right?"

I broke eye contact, not knowing if my next words were true or not. "As far as I know."

"That's what I thought." Dink grinned as he shook the ice in his cup, tilted his drink back, and guzzled the last of it. "Anyway, it'll be fun to watch Bruce squirm."

"What about Seth?"

"What about him?"

"What about his feelings in all this?"

Dink settled in his seat with a sigh. "Alex, I don't want to be a dick about this."

Dick. Dink? Pretty close.

"Here's the deal," he continued. "I don't know Seth enough to care about his feelings."

"You don't know me."

His lips lifted in that adorable smile I was starting to hate.

"True, but I want to." His hand engulfed mine completely, and by gosh, chills traveled straight up my arm and sent tingles spreading over my shoulders and neck.

Traitor, I told my body as I pulled away and folded my hands in my lap. "I don't see what the difference is."

"Are you serious?" Dink's lips twitched like he was about to laugh at any moment, but he held back. "Let's just say girls get different perks than guys."

God I was an idiot for him having to say that.

"You're blushing," he said.

"Thanks for noticing." My head heated until my scalp prickled.

"I like it. It's a sexy cute." Color actually rose to Dink's face as he dug into his dessert—an apple tart with crumbs on the top, which had me wanting to go back for my own pastry treat.

I glanced at him then away. Guilt washed over me at my not so loyal internal response. I wanted to hate him for his nonchalant attitude about my friend. Really I did… but damn. His honesty was refreshing after living a life of lies with Seth. Sure, I would have liked Dink to care about my friend's feelings, but I couldn't fault him when I had an instant dislike for any girl who wanted to sink her claws into my BFF. My same sex-counterparts always ranked a little lower on the likeability scale than guys. I didn't want to think about it.

"Is Dink a nickname?"

He looked up from his tart, one brow raised in amusement. "Is Alex?"

"Alexandria."

"Why Alex?"

I smiled with a shrug. "My parents wanted a boy. Your turn."

"Richard. My friends thought it would be funny to fuck with my name as a kid. Dink sort of stuck."

I gave him my own skeptical lift of a brow.

"It's better than Dick."

My earlier thoughts came to mind, and I laughed. "I guess you're right."

To hate or not to hate: That was the question. Watching his dimple work on a regular basis wouldn't be so bad. And with Seth acting whack, having the warmth of Dink around for snuggles certainly wouldn't hurt.

♥

My friend sat like a prince on a throne, one ankle resting on his knee as if being wheeled by a male orderly was an everyday thing. "Thanks for waiting for me."

I bristled. As if he expected anything less. "What choice did I have?"

"You always have a choice." He'd said it matter of fact but did he mean it?

"That's what friends do."

"Where are you parked?" the orderly asked.

"Near the lobby."

We followed the blue line in silence which was just as well. Stranger or no, I didn't want anyone in my business, not even an orderly I'd never see again. The quiet turned the walk into one of the longest in my life, each step bringing me closer to an unsympathetic Dink. I didn't want to see the accusation in his eyes, didn't want to see my tough friend—life of the party—turned into a social misfit.

Sidekick worked for me, kept me out of the spotlight but close to the action. The role would never do for Seth. Besides, who ever heard of a sidekick to a sidekick? The thought quirked my lips into a smile I couldn't resist.

Seth sighed and slipped into a lazy slump, sapping my amusement. He planted an elbow on the armrest and dropped his head in his hand. All he needed was a little drool trickling down the corner of his mouth to complete the picture.

As we approached the double doors, I quickened my steps and pressed the automatic button so the orderly could push Seth through without slowing. I moved aside as the wheelchair rolled past, and there was Dink, standing outside the hospital, on the other side of the glass windows. Waiting at the curve, his posture was all sorts of relaxed as he leaned against his car with his arms crossed.

At least the guys were comfortable with the situation, because I was a tight wad of stress. I took a deep breath, squared my shoulders, and rushed ahead, my hand shaking as I pressed the button to the next set of automatic doors. I bolted outside and held the door, not realizing until a few seconds later, I didn't have to. Heat rose to my face, but to let go would reveal my foolishness. My gaze darted to Dink, and I couldn't help the frown which warped my lips.

As still as he was, he could have been a statue. Only his eyes moved, as he fixated on Seth through lowered lashes. Despite saying he didn't care, the twist of his lips said otherwise. Dink pushed off the car and walked around the rear to the driver's side.

"This you?" the orderly asked.

Seth raised an eyebrow at me.

Tongue gone numb, I could only nod.

Seth leaned forward. A quick intake of air and a clutch of his stomach brought the orderly to his side. I took note of the care taken to lift my friend to his feet, and wandered if I had the strength to do the same.

Seth hunched over as he hobbled to the car. I cringed with him, reliving the kick to the gut. At that moment, I wanted nothing more than to take a baseball bat to Bruce and repay the injury. I remembered myself and sped past Seth, opening the passenger door.

He stopped in front, his face worn. My pillar of strength. Today, he didn't seem as tall as usual. "You sure?"

"Of course," I said. How could he think I'd want anything but the best for him?

Seth looked over the hood, and I followed his gaze to Dink. Our chauffeur's expression held no animosity, but it left me uncomfortable not being able to read him. I still had a hard time getting over his less than welcoming attitude toward my friend. But what did I expect? If being gay were so easy, Seth would have come out long ago.

"Well. Let's go." Dink got into the car. A few moments later, the engine turned over.

Seth stepped away from the passenger door, his face scrunching as he opened the back. "How about you take shotgun?"

"Okay." I didn't blame him. Dink wasn't mister angry-face, but he certainly wasn't mister come-right-in.

I waited for Seth to get inside before closing the door. Through the tinted glass, I could make out his heavy breathing and clenched teeth. I returned to the orderly and retrieved the brown bag full of meds—Seth's only souvenirs from his hospital visit. "Thanks."

"No problem." The orderly gave a waving salute and returned inside the building.

I took a few cleansing breath, got inside the car, and focused on the nothingness in front of me.

"We good?" In my peripheral, Dink was focused on the same nothingness.

"Yeah," I said.

"Great." Dink put the car in drive, and we were on our way, cruising through the parking lot at a far more reasonable pace than when we'd arrived at o-dark-thirty last night.

As much as I wanted to relax, my spine remained rigid. Three worries chase the peace from my mind: Dink disliking Seth, Bruce hating Seth, and a future fling with Dink. By the time we rolled onto campus my neck felt like it had a spike sticking in the base.

Dink pulled in front of Seth's dorm. I don't know how Dink knew where Seth lived, but it bothered me to think that Seth had been spending his downtime with others while leaving me out. Stupid to be jealous, for sure, but constantly competing for Seth's attention did that to me. I told myself the girls didn't matter... and deep down I knew it was true, but any attention given to a guy was genuine. It was impossible for me to deny otherwise.

I narrowed my eyes at Dink as his earlier question came to mind—*it's not like he's into me or anything, right?*—followed by my uncertain denial. Dink may not be down with gay love, but that wouldn't stop

Seth from staring at him lovingly like he had Bruce. The adoration in those baby blues belonged to me.

Dink shifted in his seat and rested his arm over my headrest. He scowled as he searched my face then blinked before his brows lifted.

I swallowed and drew back my bitterness, willed my face into neutral. Dink didn't deserve my misplaced hatred after all his help.

He cleared his throat and nodded his head to the backseat, but his eyes, full of wariness, remained locked on mine. "Do you need help?"

"No," Seth and I said in unison. I released a sigh of relief before guilt and anger bombarded me. Guilt for being too selfish to ask for help for my hurting friend. Anger because Dink had made my BFF feel unwelcomed enough to issue a rejection.

"Thanks." I diverted my eyes and got out of the car.

Dink followed suit and crossed his arms on the hood. My gaze stopped just below his chin. I couldn't force my eyes any higher, not with my emotions running rampant like a team without a coach. I gave up the pretense and opened the back door.

"I'll stop by tomorrow," Dink said.

"Okay?" I glanced at Dink's face, lingered on his wavering smile. The boy was still trying, and I couldn't help but admire his persistence. I returned the smile and hoped it didn't resemble a grimace. "Sure."

Seth eased his long legs out the car. His eyes pled with mine, yet he said nothing. He didn't have to, I'd been with him long enough to read the silent communication. I grabbed him under the elbow and pulled him to his feet. Though he stifled the groan, it still came out loud and clear, and I mentally kicked myself for not remembering to use the techniques the orderly had.

"I can help," Dink said.

Seth gave a sharp shake of his head.

"No, but thanks," I translated.

Dink rapped the roof of the car with his knuckles. "Suit yourself."

"Ready?" I asked.

"Yeah." Seth didn't look back as I escorted him to the building, but I did... more than once.

I opened the dorm door for Seth and assisted him over the threshold. As the door eased shut behind us, Dink remained in the same spot, resting against the hood of the car. It was an odd sensation... being something other than invisible. I liked it.

Chapter 8

♥

"I don't understand what the big deal is. You couldn't hide forever," I said coming out of Seth's bathroom. I took up residence next to him on the bed, snuggling close and enjoying his warmth. It was wrong, taking advantage of my best friend's forced bed rest, but I couldn't stop myself. Strike that. I didn't *want* to stop myself... not when moments with him were fleeting. Once word spread across campus, those guys not too self-conscious about hiding their true nature would come knocking at my baby's door.

Seth failed to respond to my last comment.

I tried to outlast him, but silence filled the room until it screamed for me to break it. "At least you don't have to worry about Cheyenne anymore."

"Right." The word dripped with sarcasm as he stretched it out, the 't' ending in a staccato note.

"It'll blow over." I shrugged. "You're not the first gay guy on campus."

"You don't get it, do you?" he barked out the words like I had a case of the stupids. "You know why you never hear about gay sport stars until after they retire? Because if anyone found out, no one would want them in the locker rooms. Everyone would be wondering if the gay dude is checking out their dicks or something. Like I care about every homophobe's dick. Come on!"

Baseball had been a major part of my friend's life since forever. Seth... something other than the all-star American. I hadn't wanted to consider anything past the fact I had my boy back. "I'm sorry. I didn't think—"

"Forget it. It's not your fault," Seth said, yet I couldn't help but feel partially responsible.

I should have looked out for him. If I hadn't let Dink whisk me away, perhaps Seth's secret would still be hush-hush. I'd encouraged Seth to come out of the closet, sure, but I never expected him to get beaten. No one deserved that.

My stomach dipped as I realized bruised ribs and a trip to the hospital might not be the last of the abuse. "What are you going to do about Bruce? I don't understand why you won't press charges."

"I don't want to talk about this right now."

I flinched. We talked about everything. It didn't matter if we were down and out. We were a team, leaned on one another.

"Do you think I can get some alone time?" Seth hit me with the ultimate blow.

"Are you sure?"

Seth untangled from me and rolled to his side with a grunt, giving me his back. "I could use a little something to eat."

I couldn't determine if what he said was true of if he was just trying to get rid of me—the latter I suspected. Either way, his last two comments meant I was leaving. I eased off the bed. "Sure thing."

I opened the door and Seth said, "Lock up on your way out."

My hand froze on the knob. "You'll have to get up when I return."

"You know... I'd rather sleep than eat." Seth reached behind him and flipped the bedspread over him. "Don't worry about the food. I'll see you tomorrow."

And just like that, the chasm widened like a scene in an apocalyptic movie.

♥

When I returned to my room, Framed singing *Life is an Uphill Battle* on the radio did nothing to bolster my spirits. I plopped on the bed, and the springs bounced me until they settled into place.

I never imagined Seth coming out of the closet would propel our friendship into a downward spiral. I alone knew the true him... even the secret he'd chosen to hide.

Seth should have come to me long ago, told me about Bruce. We could have worked things out together. I could have steered him toward someone more suitable... not that I hung around any other gay guys... but still. BFF meant forever, yet Seth treated forever like it only occurred during good times. Goodbye BFF, hello FWF—my fair weather friend.

A rap at the door stopped my descent into depression. *Seth?* Foolish to hope, for sure, but I did anyway. Resisting the urge to leap for the door, I called, "it's open."

The door swung inward, revealing the redheaded Goliath. Of all the people I wanted to see, Dink definitely was low on the list. With little choice now that I'd let the giant in, I put on the face of cheer. My cheeks bunched in a semblance of a smile which I didn't feel.

Dink's largeness filled the entrance. "Thought you might like to get something to eat."

I need to get something for Seth were the first words which popped into my head then reality hit. Seth hadn't wanted food; he'd just wanted me to leave.

In times of stress, I'd always had Seth. A self-professed loner, sure I was, but a loner with a friend. At least until Seth had put distance between us. I was dying inside dealing with this new depth of loneliness.

Dink knocked on the door jam, recapturing my attention. "You. Me. Food?"

I rose, grasping at the friendship Dink offered and hoping it might drag me out of my desolation. "Maybe something quick."

A slow smile lit Dink's face as he stepped to the side, letting me pass. He closed the door and rested his hand on the small of my back. At first I pretended he was Seth, the possessive hold a reaffirmation I belonged to him and would always be his friend and he mine. But the warmth of Dink's hand soon developed a moistness, making me want to pull away.

We hit the college cafeteria, and Dink piled his tray high with too many of my favorites: fries, pizza, a cheeseburger, ice cream, and more. For the first time, I realized what my parents meant by too much of a good thing. I opted for a salad, fruit bowl, and ice cream, choosing to live vicariously through Dink. I tried to reason a boy had to eat—and what a boy he was with his height and weight—but as much as I loved those goodies, the thought of eating them all in one sitting made me feel heavy and sluggish.

Dink ate with the same fervor as he had in the hospital, while I picked at my salad before moving to fruit. A bite or two later, I pushed it aside and settled on the comfort of ice cream.

Dink lifted a brow at me from time to time. Perhaps he expected me to say something or maybe he had something he wanted to get off his chest. Thankfully he kept quiet. I didn't want to talk about my problems or Seth's. Dink wouldn't understand. Heck. *I* hadn't completely wrapped my head around what was going on with my friend. Seth was supposed to be my sympathetic ear, yet here I sat with The Red Goliath in the midst of a chow down session. Best friends forever. Yeah, right. My resentment grew by the moment.

Dink tossed his napkin on his plate. "I'm thinking you might want to sit in on some of the practices... be my private cheerleader."

Private cheerleader. The role I played for Seth at his games. If he thought his baseball run was over, so was my job as his one-girl cheer squad.

"Well?" Dink grinned, oozing that teddy bear charm.

I shrugged and managed a half-smile despite secretly wanting to wallow in the misery which was mine alone. "I'll think about it."

My lackluster response was met with a pregnant pause which I did my best to ignore as I dove back into my ice cream.

"Hey," Dink said.

My spoon froze half-way to my mouth. I met his green eyes, letting the citrine centers mesmerize me. The smile which gave him an air of cuteness faded and with it the dimple I couldn't help but admire.

He leaned forward and did a quick survey of the room before returning his attention to me. "If you want, bring Seth too. I've got nothing against him."

I wanted to believe Dink. Only problem, I couldn't shake the fact he'd lowered his voice as if we were meeting on the QT and conspiring on how to get the answers for the final exams.

"I guess," I said.

"No pressure." He straightened. "I just want to get to know you a little better. That's all."

"You do?" I'd long since resigned myself to being invisible. No one other than Seth had ever wanted to know me.

"Of course."

"Why?" Yeah. Stupid question. A five-year-old would have done better asking why the sky was blue. By Dink's raised eyebrow, he thought so too.

"I mean…" I scrambled to find a more intelligent question. "Why not someone else?" *Not much better, Alexandria.*

Dink's lashes lowered as he caressed me with his gaze like he was trying out for an Ian Somerhalder role. My body warmed to the point sweat threatened to roll down my spine.

Dink chuckled. "I don't understand your obsession with Seth. You'd do a lot better, if you ditched him."

The sexy heat he'd caused in me turned dark. I stood, planted my hands on the table. "Seth and I have been friends since elementary school. You think I'm going to leave him out to dry because you don't like that he's gay?"

Dink's hands rose as if he were warding off whatever would come next. "That's not what I mean. It's just with you lapping after him no one wants to step in."

I slapped my hand against the table. "I don't lap after him."

Dink raised a golden brow.

Locked in a stare down, I wanted so much for Dink to drop his gaze. He didn't. Instead, questions raced through my head. Had I been that obvious? Had Seth picked up on it? The answers were apparent even if I didn't want to face them. I'd seen it in Seth's eyes when he denied my request to play his pretend girlfriend.

I hated that I broke eye contact first and resigned myself to slinking in my chair.

"You're so busy keeping an eye on your friend, you never notice anyone watching you," Dink said. Some people couldn't leave well enough alone.

"If you say so."

"Seriously."

"Riiight."

"Fine." Dink shrugged. "Don't believe me."

I stared at my melting ice cream, a smile flexing my cheeks. Could I—the wall flower—really have been noticed? A fresh dose of entitlement hit me. Seth may not have acknowledged me as girlfriend material, but others had. "You think so?"

Dink's hand enveloped mine, and I met his eyes.

"Yeah... I do." All humor had fled his face, locking me in time. I was trapped in his gaze, even as nervousness urged me to pull from his grasp, hide in a corner, and blend into a wall. But I didn't want to withdraw, not when rejecting Dink meant I'd be alone without Seth again.

♥

"Where have you been?" Seth asked when I returned to his room hours later.

I avoided eye contact, my time with Dink filling me with the shame of betrayal. "Getting something to eat."

"Took you long enough."

I walked to his bed, bag in outstretched hand. "I got your favorites."

"Good, I'm starving." He grabbed the paper bag, taking no preliminaries as he dug out a chicken sandwich. "I thought you'd never get back."

I plopped on the edge of his bed and crossed my arms. "I thought you didn't want me around."

"Don't be such a drama queen." Seth bit into his sandwich.

Drama queen—like him freaking out in the hospital. Sure, let him get all pissy and take his frustrations out on me when it wasn't even my fault, but when I got upset over the way he treated me, then *I'm* the drama queen.

"I was with Dink," I blurted for no other reason than to prove his rejection didn't leave me sulking in a corner of miserable solitude.

Seth took another bite. Only the slight twitch of his nose indicated my statement held any significance for him.

"He wants to spend more time with me." Petty? Yes. But I couldn't help the sick sense of satisfaction which filled me to bursting. Someone other than Seth valued my presence, wanted to hang out with me.

"That's nice," Seth said between bites.

I smiled. My boy couldn't pull off nonchalance with me. Dare I play along? "I might sit in on a few of his games... maybe go to some of the practices."

Seth swallowed, ducking his head as if trying to force the chunk down his esophagus.

I wanted to feel bad about the barbs, but he was the one who'd told me to get lost. He was the one who'd opened me up to Dink's attentions.

Seth cleared his throat and searched the room.

"Want me to get you a drink?" I asked.

He nodded. I went to the mini-fridge, grabbed a soda, and returned. A few check marks appeared on my mental scoreboard under my name and more than made up for losing the stare down with Dink.

A few gulps later and Seth set his drink aside. "I don't think the guys would appreciate me watching them on the field."

"You don't have to come with me." I shrugged. "I know how busy you get sometimes."

Seth rewrapped his sandwich and shoved it back in the bag.

"There's ice cream too." I berated myself for not putting the frozen treat in the freezer.

"Not really in the mood." He leaned back, putting on the pouty face he'd perfected over the years. "I didn't think you were that into sports."

"After watching you on the diamond for how long?" I slapped him on the leg. "You've got to be kidding me."

"Why do you want to hang out with them anyway?"

I wanted to crawl away from Seth's glare. Instead I let my gaze drop as my courage to bait my friend faded. "I don't want to hang around them." —*Truth.* "I wouldn't mind getting to know Dink a little better." —*Blatant lie.* "He's been nice to me... the only one who offered to take you to the hospital."

"Fine." Seth reached into the bag again and retrieved his ice cream along with the spoon. "I just didn't get the impression you were so into him."

Seemed the transparency went both ways when it came to our friendship. If that were the case, Dink and the rest of the world weren't the only ones who realized I had the hots for my BFF. Seth had been onto me all along. I burned with the shame of his earlier rejection.

Perhaps dating Dink would be best... a way to cover the nakedness of my desire. I could give Dink a chance; I should.

"No one likes ice cream sludge." Seth tilted the cup toward me. Neapolitan goop. It even looked warm.

"You didn't even want it." I took the ice cream from him along with his bag of trash and crossed the room to the wastebasket.

"That was before."

"Oh please."

"I don't think Dink is right for you."

I dropped the garbage in the basket and faced Seth—my golden boy BFF whom I loved. The pretty boy who saw me as nothing more than the girl he grew up with. My heart twinged as if I suffered from an arrhythmia. "What do you know about what's right for me?"

The truth of my love flashed between us, yet there were no words to be said. I'd known we'd reach this impasse one day when I'd first discovered my feelings had grown beyond friendship. I just hadn't wanted to admit how impossible the situation would be.

I walked to the door. "I need to study."

"Alex, wait."

I pulled the door shut behind me, thankful he was too incapacitated to chase after. The tears flowed freely long before I reached the stairwell. Heads turned my way, but at least my blurred vision kept me from seeing the pity on their faces.

Chapter 9

♥

When the first rays of sunlight pricked through the blinds, I was too tired to rise... too depressed to get up even if I did have the energy. Hours later, I rolled to the side and coaxed my body out of bed.

The clock blipped nine forty-two.

Go to him. Make sure he's okay, a small voice in my head said.

It took entirely too long to drag myself to the shower, and the warm water did nothing to wash away my weariness.

Thoughts of Seth lying in bed, too sore to move to get a decent meal pushed me to trudge over to his place. I knocked on his door, worry plaguing me when he didn't answer. Then I realized despite all the chaos of the weekend, Monday had arrived right on schedule. Seth would be in Quantum Mechanics. Even worse, I'd overslept and missed my first class and half of the second.

Realization shot a burst of energy into me. This time I sprinted. Back in my room, I grabbed my books. My legs couldn't move fast enough as I raced to class. *One absence wasn't that big of a deal.* Only, I'd heard too many horror stories of students flunking out of school because the material on the tests was given from the lectures rather than the text.

Outside the statistics classroom, I took two deep breaths, brushed the sweat from my brow, and opened the door. All eyes turned to me. And with fifteen minutes left of class, why shouldn't they?

"Excuse me, Miss..." The instructor pushed up his glasses. A class this size, I wasn't surprised Mr. Dober didn't know my name.

"Carmichael. Alexandria Carmichael." I tried not to roll my eyes with the James Bond introduction.

"Miss Carmichael, please remember what time class starts."

"Yes, sir." I headed to the closest empty seat.

"You're excused."

I froze halfway between sitting and standing. "What?"

"You're excused. Class started —" he looked at his watch "— an hour and three minutes ago. I'd appreciate if you not interrupt my class again."

A few snickers in the background and my temperature went up a few notches as I backtracked to the exit. "I'm sorry."

I stepped out of the room and pulled the door shut with a soft click. *No big deal. No big deal,* I tried to tell myself as I leaned against the wall, but for some reason, my pep talk wasn't strong enough to keep the tears from flowing. My shoes clapped against the linoleum as I rushed to the bathroom. I hated crying. Already I imagined my eyes turning tight and dry after all was said and done.

Twice in a twenty-four hour period. A dribble of snot trickled over my lips as I pushed open the door to the restroom. The only upside was that everyone was in class, allowing me to cry in solitude.

To be honest, I didn't even care about getting kicked out of class. It was only the tipping point. No matter how hard I tried, the world plotted against me.

I washed my face and was in the process of drying with a paper towel when the door opened, letting in the sound of the bustling students in the hallway.

The dismissal of class announced lunch time for me. I hefted my bag over my shoulder.

"Got eye drops?" The cackle which followed froze me in place. Cheyenne stepped behind me, filling the mirror with her presence and her god awful smirk.

What I would do to slap that smile off her face. I turned to her, my hands itching, my eyes burning with tears threatening to fall.

She blinked, and her brows creased with uncertainty. Suddenly she wasn't worth the effort. All the fight drained out of me, and I walked away like the loser I was.

Fighting had become too hard... too exhausting. I walked under the weight of it all—one foot after the other, each step coming a little slower. It seemed like a year had passed before I reached my room. I collapsed on my bed and wrapped the bedspread around me. Let the world take care of itself... Seth could take care of *himself* for that matter. I needed to take care of me before the world did me in.

♥

The knock at my door came after nightfall. I didn't answer. After all, the prospects at the door weren't great: either Dink asking me if I want to watch him shovel food into his face, Seth with the never-ending letdowns, or some school administrator coming to reprimand me for skipping class today.

"Can we at least talk?" Seth said from the other side.

The "talk" played in my head—Seth sitting in the chair, me on the bed. He'd start by prattling about the longevity of our friendship before going into his gay status. We'd have a *duh* moment. He'd smile like everything was okay, the past blunders of our relationship forgotten. I'd smile back, but only to hide my broken heart. No... not going to happen. I lacked the strength to fake what I didn't feel, and I was tired of pretending.

"A break would be nice after the long walk." Seth let weakness seep into his voice.

Jerk. Leave it to him to find the right combination to bend me to his will. I unlocked the door without opening it and returned to bed, flopping facedown.

The chaotic voices of the students in the hall followed Seth inside before he closed the door with a soft click, muting the noise.

"Alex?" Seth approached, and the bed dipped as he sat on the edge. "I'm sorry about yesterday."

I pulled the feigned sleep tactic like my friend had done in the hospital. One problem: tears moistened the corners of my eyes. I didn't move as Seth affixed earpieces around my lobes. Music floated through—Sway by The Perishers. By the time the lyrics hit the chorus I'd drenched my pillow, filling the room with hiccupy sobs. All the while, Seth rubbed small circles on my back.

The song faded with an apology and a request. Could I be his solid ground?

I didn't know any more. I wanted to be. I wished I could turn back the clock to a time when we were just buddies, Seth was the closet gay, and I kept my love for him secret. Openness wasn't as golden as I'd once thought. *Hindsight is twenty-twenty*, my mother had said too many times.

Even after the tears stopped, the sniffles continued. By then, Seth had moved on to stroking my hair.

"If you date Dink, I won't crimp your style." Seth offered the consolation prize as if it was a worthy tradeoff. "You deserve someone wonderful."

Did that mean he thought Dink was that 'someone wonderful' or was he hinting I deserved better?

"You probably want to be alone."

I didn't, but I did.

"I just wanted to say I'm sorry." The bed leveled as he stood, and his footsteps drifted away. The door opened but didn't close. "I don't deserve to have a say, considering the way I've been acting, but I miss you… a lot. If you're up to it, if you can forgive me, maybe we can meet up after class tomorrow and go to dinner. Like old times?"

I sat, wiped the tears, and breathed deeply before taking in his hopeful face. "I'd like that."

He nodded. He didn't suggest staying, and I didn't ask. Rather he shut the door on his way out, giving us an opportunity to start fresh.

My vision blurred with new tears. We were beyond fresh starts. Like a cracked baseball bat, the structural integrity of our relationship had weakened.

Chapter 10

♥

Avoiding statistics forever wasn't an option, at least not if I wanted to pass. I rocked from toe to heel, my anxiety increasing with every second as students from the prior class filtered out. Invisible worked usually. Today, I'd settle on being a nobody amongst the masses.

The flow dwindled to a trickle, and I darted inside, eager to have my pick of seats. I chose one near the back. Inconspicuous was the game I'd play until the instructor forgot I was the doofus who'd showed up fifteen minutes before class had ended a couple of days earlier.

"Hey. I'm Trinity Webber." A black girl, hair no longer than the first joint of my pinkie, took the seat beside me.

"Alex—"

"Carmichael." She smiled. "I remember."

I sighed as I slumped in my chair. "Wonderful."

Trinity laughed. "Don't worry about it. I doubt Dober even remembers you."

Or so I hoped.

"Even if he does, it's better to stand out than fade to the background." Trinity scowled at the back of Mr. Dober's head.

He turned around, and Trinity attracted his attention with a friendly wave. Mr. Dober nodded with a smile before returning to the formula on the smart board.

"See." Trinity gave a knowing smile. "And if he remembers my name, even better."

"If you say so."

"I do." Her eyes twinkled with mischief. "A few brownie points would have done you some good yesterday."

"Thanks for rubbing it in."

"No problem." She winked.

Oh. She's good. Just like the old Seth. I didn't have time to get mad as she yanked the irritation out of the situation.

"You know the points accumulate, right?"

I lifted an eyebrow.

"Like that wave was good for the beginning of class." Trinity lowered her voice. "But if I chat up a teacher before the start, it'd be extra points. Lucky for us, I've been sending him waves like clockwork since the first day of school."

I frowned. "What?"

"I'll show you." She scooted her chair closer and rested her elbow on the table. For the next hour and twenty minutes she rambled non-stop.

The instructor zeroed in on me a few times and gave me the evil eye as if I had some kind of control over Trinity's ever-moving lips, but not once did he say a word. No doubt, he would have called me out like he'd done yesterday if I'd pulled a stunt like her.

Plenty of personality flowed from Trinity. I could lose myself in her shadow so easily... like with Seth. But a shadow was nothing without the body.

Right as the instructor ended the lecture, Trinity took me by surprise with, "what do you have planned after class?"

I stared at her. She had the darkest eyes—darker even than mine. Unfathomable. She eclipsed me, drew me in the way Seth did.

I didn't want to fall into that role again, become an extension of another person. It hurt too much. "I—"

"I mean..." She looked away. "I'm new on campus and haven't made any friends. I didn't mean to impose or come on too strong." She glanced back at me. "You just seemed a bit bummed, and I thought... I'm such a moron. I sound like a fifth grader."

Trinity scooped up her books and stood.

"Wait." I grabbed her forearm. "I'm sort of short on friends also."

A slow smile curled her lips. "We'll make quite the dynamic duo."

I cringed internally, imagining myself in the role of Robin... once again the sidekick.

"Strike that," she said, extending her hand to me. "I'm thinking more like partners in crime."

Partners. I rather liked that. It had an air of equality I'd not experienced since that fateful day in first grade. I took her hand, gave it a firm shake. "That works for me."

"Thought so." She wagged her brows, and her grip tightened as she pulled me to my feet. "Lunch time."

Very seldom had I encountered a person shorter than me—not including children of course. Trinity was definitely shorter than my five-one. The awkward sensation of staring down instead of up left me wondering if people felt uncomfortable standing next to me. Two little munchkins.

As if reading my mind, Trinity linked her arm with mine and hummed to the tune of *We Represent the Lollipop Guild.* I couldn't help but laugh as she dragged me out the classroom.

Chapter 11

♥

"I wish I'd brought a blanket. This bench is freezing," I said.

In the past, Seth would have squeezed closer and wrapped his arm around me. Today? Nothing. Just silence as he sat with his elbows on his knees, shoulders slumped.

I couldn't be sure if he was grumpy about watching the football team practice or saddened his secret affections toward Bruce had come to an end. Perhaps a little of both. He probably should have stayed in his dorm room.

More than a week had passed since the incident. His body was almost healed, the bruises yellowing, but the emotional and psychological impact seemed as fresh as ever. He hadn't been the same since. Neither had our relationship.

Gone was the outgoing boy who dragged me to event after event. In his place was a sullen guy who carried a cloud of gloom about him, dampening any semblance of happiness I might glean from landing my first boyfriend.

Dink. Caving to the persistent red-haired Goliath hadn't been easy, but he eased the loneliness as Seth withdrew into himself a little more each day.

"Why did you come?" I wasn't being mean with the question, but Mr. Glum wasn't exactly the life of the party.

"What else do I have to do?"

Catch up on the school work you missed yesterday because of your follow-up appointment. I pursed my lips tight against the words which wanted to escape.

The clatter of football equipment as the guys collided on the field drew my attention. Other than numbers, they all looked the same to me, but something about the players clashing together was totally sexy in a way baseball had never been. Sure baseball put the players in those tight uniforms which revealed all, but the physical contact... nom nom. The primitiveness of it all sent my heart racing, drew me to the edge of my seat.

The team did one last huddle and broke away with a *hoo-yah* and migrated to the locker rooms, while Dink made a beeline toward the bleachers… or rather me. One other guy held back, helmet still on his head. *Bruce*.

Was he peeved Seth sat next to me, playing the part of the creeper?

Dink pulled off his helm and clanked it against the metal bleachers as he leaned forward. "I'll pick you up at seven. We'll hang out at Gretel's."

I turned to Seth who seemed fixated on Bruce idling on the field before I returned my attention to Dink.

"A lot of the guys from the team will be there." His gaze locked with mine, not even acknowledging the presence of my BFF.

I gave Dink points for laying the choice out in an ever so subtle way: him or Seth. Under different circumstances the answer would be clear—Seth before all and certainly before the consolation prize of my Goliath boyfriend.

Was this the way Seth had felt all those times, pretending to romance girls? Now, I was the player, and I hated myself a little because of it.

"Well?" Dink asked.

"I don't know." My gaze slid to my friend.

Seth stood. "You should go. I've got stuff to do." Rather than hopping straight down the bleachers from bench to bench, he took the long way to the steps using the guardrail like he might slip and break a hip at any moment.

I focused on the heart line of my palm, unable to bear watching Seth walk away as if he was leaving me behind forever.

Dink climbed the bleachers, shaking the stands with every step, and sat beside me, dropping his helmet between his feet. "You okay?"

"I guess." I replayed parts of the practice in my head to keep from focusing on the tears threatening to surface. I'd let Dink into my life to fill an empty hole, only to find that gap growing daily.

Absence makes the heart grow fonder. Not really. The further Seth and I grew apart, the more independent I became. The more I realized I'd survive without him. And that hurt the most.

What would Seth think if he knew about my developing friendship with Trinity, that I ate lunch with her every day... that we laughed and joked the way Seth and I had before Rush.

"If you want, we can do something else. We don't have to hang with the guys." Dink's palm fell heavy on my thigh, massaging and sending pleasant warmth up my leg. I could almost pretend the hand was Seth's, save for the meatiness and dirt embedded under the nails.

Seth was too conscientious to let grime accumulate. If manicures were kosher for men, my boy would have been in the salon weekly.

The wrongness of substituting Dink for Seth put a kink in my stomach, made it difficult to keep my mouth from twisting in distaste.

I stood and brushed the smudge of dirt Dink left on my jeans. "No. That's okay. Seven you said?"

"You sure?" Dink's lips curled into a sheepish smile.

I so wanted to press my finger into the indentation on his cheek. "Yeah. I'll be ready."

"With most of the guys at Gretel's, the house will be close to empty." He grabbed my hand, enclosing me in the rough dryness of his.

Poor Dink. He made my choice so easy. Dating him was no problem, but anything further did not jive. My heart still belonged to Seth, and I didn't want to deal with trying to fend off the advances of my fake boyfriend... not tonight.

I took a step down the bleachers, then another. My fingertips lingered against his before I pulled away. "Seven o'clock. Gretel's."

Like Seth, I didn't look back.

♥

Dink drove with one hand on the steering wheel, the other on my right knee. After a while, I had to remind myself not to pull away as his palm grew hot and humid.

Ten more minutes and we'll be at Gretel's, I encouraged myself.

How had Seth pretended for so long? After a week, I'd already grown tired of the façade but was clueless on how to end the relationship.

Seth tended to drift until most girls got the picture and broke up with him, but Dink didn't seem to care that I'd never shown true interest. After a week of dating, I'd learned little more about him than his class schedule... and the fact he liked to eat.

My consciousness beat at me for not being forthcoming from the beginning, but loneliness made me selfish. *Come back to me*, I sent the psychic whisper to my best friend, wishing upon wishes he could hear my call.

The ride continued in silence—a typical evening with Dink. He pulled into a parking garage close to Gretel's and circled to the third level before squeezing into a tight spot.

"We're here." He twisted in his seat and gave me his full attention. "Sure you don't want to hang out at the Alpha house?"

His hand traveled up my thigh, helping me lock in my answer. "No. It's nice to escape the campus."

Dink sighed before getting out. My mother often said a guy should open the car door for his girlfriend, but she was old school. Plus, I kind of didn't want Dink doing anything for me... not when breaking up with him probed my thoughts. By the time he came to the passenger side, I was already slamming the door shut.

I let Dink put his arm around me all the while hating that I only reached armpit high. With him, the small things irked me. Still I tried to take advantage of his warmth as we walked to Gretel's, letting his bulk block the chill of the wind.

Dink opened the door, and the loudness reached a level I'd never experienced in the small restaurant. The place was packed, filled with faces I recognized from the football team and cheer squad.

Cheyenne popped up from her chair like a whac-a-mole. How I wished I had a mallet. She waved to Dink... and I guess me, since I was attached to his side. "Over here."

Dink's hand slipped to my waist as he guided me to a table with Bruce, Bill, Cheyenne and three other cheerleaders I'd seen on the field but never took the time to learn their names. My fake boyfriend pulled out a chair and waited ever so patiently until I got the hint the seat was for me.

"Thank you." I sat, feeling girlish and loving the extra attention. As nice as Dink was, he deserved someone who returned his affections... someone other than me.

Before Dink took the seat beside me, Cheyenne's lips were already moving. "So where's Seth?"

Her sudden question sent a shock through my system. My throat tightened, refused a single breath. The girl had a lot of nerve bringing up my friend as if she had any interest.

"Let's just have a good time and not talk about Seth," Dink said. I secretly thanked him for answering.

"I'm sure everyone is as curious as me." Queen Cheerleader met the gazes of her drones before fixating on Bruce, but Seth's love interest remained as stoic as ever.

"Anywayzzz." Cheyenne rolled her eyes to me. "Where is fagboy?"

The crack of flesh against flesh caused more than a few to jerk in their seats. I stared at Cheyenne in stunned silence as the cheerleader's hand flew to her cheek, reddened skin peeking between her fingers. Even more surprising was my stinging palm which sparkled. It took me awhile to recognize the glitters for what they were... her makeup.

My hand shook, and my shoulder hurt a little from overextending it. The restaurant grew too bright in a surreal sort of way, making those at the table go in and out of focus. Half of them pinned wide-eyes on me; the other dangled their mouths as they focused on Cheyenne.

Her eyes glistened; mine would have too. She rose, and her chair fell backward with a crash. Cheyenne raced toward the exit, her quick steps just shy of a run. Nobody said anything as the door ease shut behind her. Then as one, all eyes turned to me.

"Seth needed to study," I said but wasn't sure why the words left my lips. The only thing I knew for certain was I had one heck of an adrenaline high which left me more than a little dizzy. "I think I better go."

My chair scraped against the floor as I stood. Soon enough I realized I didn't have a ride. Dink hadn't bothered to move, though his brows seemed fixed in a furrow as if he didn't recognize me.

"I'll call a cab," I said.

Dink blinked once. Twice. A third time. "No. I'll take you."

"Thanks," I managed, too numb to say anything else. One thought echoed in my head: *she didn't hit me back*.

♥

Anger rolled off Dink, filling the car with heat. I wanted to roll down a window, turn on the air conditioning, anything to relieve the flush, but I didn't want to draw attention to myself.

Dink kept his eyes fixed on the road, his hands at two and ten. My dad did that on days when I screwed up, and he didn't know how to handle the situation.

Keep your hands to yourself, my mother had told me on more than one occasion. But she'd also said, *if you can't say anything nice, don't say anything at all*—advice Cheyenne missed somewhere along the line. She should have known better. No. *I* should have known better than to hang out with a bunch of Dink's friends. I didn't belong with that crowd.

"I'd like to go to Seth's dorm," I said.

Dink stiffened, his hands tightening around the steering wheel until the knuckles whitened along the edges. "Fine."

"Thank you."

"I'm sorry about Cheyenne." Eyes locked on the road, his head didn't even nudge my way.

I didn't know what to make of his comment. Was he not mad at me? I did the only thing I could think of... remained silent.

Dink's car pulled to the curb, and I jerked back into the seat as I tried to leave without unfastening my belt. A bit of fumbling and I managed to get out of the car, my entire body burning with embarrassment.

I took a few steps down the walkway before Dink's door squeaked open.

"Alex," he called.

I froze. Indecision rode me as I debated if stopping sufficed or if I needed to face him. The silence which followed clued me in, and I turned around. "Yeah."

"If you want to do something... just the two of us, maybe I can pick you up after classes tomorrow."

I don't think that is best was my instant reaction, but the hopeful lift of his brows made me feel guilty I'd given him hope at all.

"What did you have in mind?" I asked, wanting to renege the moment the words left my mouth.

He smiled, and the solitary dimple in his right cheek made an appearance. "A movie?"

He's a nice guy, a small part of my brain said. It was true for the most part, but did I want to string him along until feelings which weren't there grew into something more? Standing in front of Seth's dorm, preparing to meet the cold shoulder had me nodding instead of saying, *this isn't going to work*.

"Great." Dink gave the hood his signature double tap. "I'll look up the show times and give you a call tonight."

"Yeah. Great," I mumbled as I head to the dorm. Now I was no better than the rest of the bimbos on the planet who teased and led guys on. No small wonder my friend preferred the male species. At least they gave it straight... no games. Except Seth.

Who was I kidding? Guys were just as bad.

I stepped inside Seth's dorm and waited until Dink drove away. Despite wanting to go to my BFF, I couldn't talk to him about boyfriend problems... the situation was too weird... the relationship still stressed. Resigned, I walked into the cold night and returned to my room.

Chapter 12

♥

"Again?" Seth stood between me in the bedroom, trapping me in the bathroom.

I swirled the applicator brush in my compact. "Yes, again."

"You've gone out with Dink every night this week." Seth let all sorts of pout into his voice.

"We're dating." I raised my brows, adding special emphasis on the *dating* before turning back to the mirror, sweeping blush across my cheeks.

Ugh. What a bother. I hated the caked on sensation of makeup. *A girl's gotta do what a girl's gotta do.* Especially when dating a guy she just wasn't into. "Besides... what do you care?"

He crossed his arms. "I don't."

Mr. Pouty didn't fool me. At least now he knew how I felt when he went on *his* fake dates. I pushed Seth aside and walked to the closet. "I wonder if we're going to dinner also."

Seth met my statement with silence. No problem, I had plenty of chitchat to fill the gap.

"I'm thinking about wearing this." I grabbed a cashmere cardigan from the lower shelf and tossed it on the bed.

Seth unfolded the sweater. "What are you going to put under it?"

"Me."

Seth's left eyebrow lifted.

I wagged both of mine. The low neckline was not my normal wear, considering I wasn't the show and tell kind of gal. Seth had talked me into buying the knit. I'd caved for him, one of many concessions I made in the hope he'd notice his best friend came in the form of a girl.

False hope. As far as he was concerned, I was just the model... an outlet for his fashion sense. No matter. At least I had something cute for tonight.

I grabbed a pair of form fitting jeans, placed them at my waist and did a hip tilt. "You like?"

"Sure." Seth headed toward the door. "I'll catch you later."

"You're leaving?"

Seth paused with his hand on the knob, not bothering to face me. "I doubt anyone from the football team wants to see me. Frankly, I kinda want to keep a low profile, if you know what I mean."

"Seth—"

"Don't bother." He opened the door and left me watching the hallway which seemed as vacant as the spot in my heart.

We couldn't let our friendship fade to nothing. I took quick steps to the door. Running would be silly, but I wanted to. I rounded the corner and smacked my nose into a chest. My eyes teared but I could still make out Dink.

"Sorry." He grabbed my arm and steered me back into the room. Not that I had much resistance in me with a bashed nose and all.

The back of my knees hit the bed, and my legs buckled.

Dink knelt in front of me. "God, I'm such an ass."

"It wasn't your fault." I wiped the tears from my eyes and wiggled the hurt from my nose. "You're early."

"I hope you don't mind."

I tugged my jeans from under me. "I'm not dressed."

"We don't have to go out, if you're not up to it now." His hand caressed my calf.

"No." I rose. "I'm fine."

"You sure?" His hands found their way to the back of my thighs, his mouth about crotch high.

"Uhmm." I grabbed my sweater and eased out of his hold. "I'll be right back."

This is wrong. So wrong. I rushed to the bathroom and shut the door. Letting Dink think he had a chance wasn't right. Sure he was cute with that dimple and all, but he had so many habits which irked me. My mother always said, *the little things matter the most.* Until Dink, I hadn't understood what she meant.

"I'm thinking we can go for a later show. If you haven't eaten, we can get dinner first." Dink said.

"Yeah. Sure." I hated the way he shoveled food into his mouth... and he ate so much. He wasn't disgusting or anything. It was more that he devoured food without any care in the matter. He wasn't fat, but certainly was nowhere near the lean muscle of Seth.

Seth. Would I compare every guy to my BFF from this day forth? My first boyfriend. Didn't Dink at least deserve a chance?

Chapter 13

♥

I mentally urged Dink to drive faster. He'd been one of those nonstop talkers during the movie—bad enough I had to clench my teeth to keep from telling him to shut the hell up.

Dink chuckled. He'd been doing that the entire ride home.

"What?" Only common courtesy pushed me to inquire, because by the powers that be, I was so fed up with him, I'd just as soon staple his lips together.

"Nothing," he said. "Just thinking about the movie."

Oh my gosh! I laughed to keep from crying. I'd looked forward to watching that movie with Seth. Potentially a five-star show, with Dink by my side, it turned out to be a negative three.

Dink pulled into a parking spot in front of my dorm.

"Later." I flung the door open.

"Wait." Dink got out. "I'll walk you up."

Not on your life. I rounded to his side. "I'm exhausted. How about a quick kiss" —*ugh*— "and you watch me head inside, okay?"

Dink frowned.

What he was thinking, I didn't know and frankly didn't care after he'd ruined the movie. *Come on, you lug. Let's get this over with.* I rose to my tippy toes, ready to step down after a peck.

"Yeah. Okay." Dink wrapped an arm around my waist, pulling me against him and holding me in place as he lowered his head.

I tried not to cringe as he breathed out the heavy scent of popcorn but couldn't stop my nose from crinkling.

Either he didn't notice or didn't care, because his lips still found mine. His tongue probed and bumped my teeth as he deepened the kiss. I tried to drop my heels. Instead of letting me ease to the ground, he managed my weight, and I found myself dangling in his arms.

"Wow." I pushed at his chest, gasping and hoping he thought he'd taken my breath away. "That'll give me something to remember until next we meet." *Until next we meet? Really, Alex? This isn't a cheesy scene from a soap opera.*

I backed away and waved as I turned toward the dorm. My walking jog carried me to the door where I gave one last flutter of my fingers and darted inside. Down the hall, I grabbed a candy bar from the vending machine before returning to the front.

Dink's car was nowhere in sight. *Perfect.*

I finished my chocolate goodie then crept out the dorm and cut across the parking lot. The fear of being caught by Dink helped me make haste. I was winded by the time I hit Seth's dorm and decided to take the elevators. Unlike my best friend, I never claimed to be a health addict.

Seth's door was wide open when I reach his room. Not very often did I catch his bed rumpled; he was that much of a neat freak.

"Hey." I strolled in—my right as his best friend. If Seth didn't want me to make myself at home, he should have closed the door. I smile on my way to his bathroom. *Empty.*

I did a one-eighty. Not a lot of places to hide in a studio-style room—bathroom, mini-kitchen, and bedroom. That was all.

"Seth." I returned to the front and stuck my head into the hallway. It wasn't like my friend to leave his room unsecure. I closed the door. As an uninvited guest on the inside, the owner on the out, the action tickled me wrong, and I reopen the door.

I wanted to tell Seth I was sorry for abandoning him... that going out with Dink was a mistake... that I continued to make mistakes. My friend's advice would be perfect right now. If anyone knew a way out of the Dink situation, it'd be Seth. I fell back on the bed, letting my head plop against the mattress.

A spot crinkled beneath me, and I sat, searched the wrinkled blankets, and pulled out a paper... a letter. An occasional droplet warped a few of the words, but Seth's neat print was still easy to read.

> *Dear Alex,*
>
> *Sorry I couldn't be what you wanted me to be. Believe me, I wanted to, but that's just not me. I couldn't treat you like the other girls. You've been a good friend. I've always wanted to fly. I guess I'll get my chance after all. See you on the other side.*
>
> *Love,*
> *Seth*

See you on the other side? I reread the note twice more. Everything in the letter I understood... all except for the last line. *See you on the other side.* The other side of what?

Seth's comments as he stood on the ledge returned to me. *Alex, have you ever wondered what it'd be like to fly? The wind whistling by. One moment in time.*

I jumped to my feet and ran. Students made way as I raced past. I hit the doors to the stairs at a full run and bounced off, landed hard on my butt. People snickered behind me as I rose. Common sense on my side this time, I turned the handle and took the steps two at a time, stretching my short legs to the max, tripping along the way as I misjudged the length. At the top of the stairwell, I slowed to a stop and smashed the bar on the door to the rooftop.

Seth sat in plain view, straddling the cement guard. He turned to me, and his shoulders slumped. "I figured you'd be gone longer."

"What does it matter how long I'd be gone? What are you doing, Seth?" I couldn't quite wrap my head around the fact that my suspicions were true. Seth — the coolest guy on the planet — played with suicide. The words just didn't go together.

He answered me with silence, whipped his other leg over the edge. My heart did a swan dive, bounced off my toes, and jumped to my neck. I couldn't move. I couldn't speak. I couldn't even will him not to stop. My eyes widened though I wanted to clamp them shut.

"My life is over. I'm only prolonging what needs to happen." Seth's voice broke me out of the trance.

My pounding heart made me dizzy, and I struggled to keep from falling to my knees. "How can you say that?"

My friend gave a mirthless laugh. "I don't have to listen to the gossip to know what everyone is saying."

"What are they saying?"

"I'm gay." Surely he couldn't be serious.

"Seth. You *are* gay." Doh! Foot in mouth. I was the worst person on the planet to talk someone off a rooftop and berated myself for not asking for help on my way up.

Fear kept me from speaking into the silence, despite lameness filling the dead air. I focused on calming my heart, which leapt to my throat every few beats, then plunged to twirl in my stomach, threatening to bring up popcorn and soda.

Seth chuckled. A real chuckle, not a joyful one, but at least it included a dose of amusement.

My confused brain signaled my face to try a smile which twitched into a grimace before fading. "What's so funny?"

"I'm gay." A moment ago the fact had put him on the rooftop. "Only you would point out the obvious and think it's okay."

Heat crept up my neck, filled my head like a hot air balloon.

He swung his legs to the side of safety. Even so, all he had to do was lean back, and it'd be over.

"You're not going to jump?" I bit my tongue. The question came out like I was surprised he'd changed his mind... as if I wanted him to follow through.

"I can't." He hopped off the barrier. "Not with you watching."

Suicide shy? A bit of hate blossomed that he could think suicide was an option but faded as relief took its place. I ran to him, wrapped my arms around his waist, letting the chill of his body cool me. The beat of his heart against my cheek reminded me how precious life was, how fleeting.

"I don't know what the big deal is," I said into his chest. "There are other gay folks on campus."

"I don't want to be 'other gay folks.'" He grabbed my biceps, putting me away from him. His eyes went crazy wide as he stared at me.

I steeled myself and hoped I didn't show how freaked out the look made me. Sociopath eyes.

"You don't get it." He brushed past. "You should have stayed out longer."

His words punched my stomach, causing it to swirl. Did that mean he'd try again?

"Seth, wait!"

He reached the door and pressed the handle. "Shit. Didn't you think to prop it open or something?"

"It's locked?" I recalled smashing the bar as I'd exited onto the rooftop.

"What do you think?"

A bit of defensive anger flared. "Why didn't *you* prop it open?"

He crossed his arms, rolled his eyes. "I was taking the other way down. Until you arrived, I was all good."

"How did this become my fault?" I wasn't sure if I should be hurt or angry.

"Forget it."

I settled on sad. "I don't understand what happened. Aren't we friends anymore?"

"Did you bring your cell phone?"

"Don't ignore me, Seth. Are we still friends? I need to know." *Only tell me if the answer is yes.*

He laid a hand over his breast. "Till death do us part."

I didn't like the finality to it.

Chapter 14

♥

"Would you prefer we not be friends?" I almost didn't want to hear the answer.

"It's not that." Seth released a weary sigh. "I just think life would be easier if I didn't have anyone to worry about me."

"I don't understand."

He shrugged. "I mean without you, who would miss me?"

"Your family."

"More people to disappoint."

"How can you think that way?" The gravel on the roof crunched beneath my shoes as I crossed the distance. "You're my best friend. I've never cared you were gay."

His lips twisted in a smirk. "So you say."

The first line of his letter: *Sorry I couldn't be what you wanted me to be.* He should have been able to freely express himself around me, but I'd wanted him to change the most. So, I didn't turn my back on him because he was gay. Big whoop-ti-do when I wanted him to love me the way a boy loved a girl. An impossibility, yet I pressured him in my little ways. *Sorry*, he'd written, but in truth I owed him.

Meeting his eyes was difficult, but I forced myself not to break contact. "I'm sorry. You shouldn't have to change for me. You've always been perfect in my mind. I think that's why—"

"Don't say it." His eyes turned shiny.

I blinked, choosing my next words carefully, but only the truth wanted to emerge. "You already know, Seth. Keeping quiet won't change the way I feel."

"What do we do?"

"I'm not sure. I want to go back to the way things were, but then I don't. It's too late. We can't go back."

Seth's brows drew together as if they yearned for a solution as much as I did.

"I'm thinking," I began. "Perhaps I can just be me, loving my best friend..." I smiled though bitterness wanted to twist my lips. "...my gay best friend, but knowing he'll always love someone else."

"I love you," Seth said like we were having an argument he had to win.

"You know what I mean."

His long golden lashes fluttered, moisture twinkling between the strands. His gaze shifted to the ground.

Despite the downer conversation, getting my feelings into the open lightened my spirit even as a twinge of guilt hit me for unburdening on Seth. God I was a shitty friend. My BFF was suicidal, and here I was, finding ways to make myself feel better and my buddy like crap. "I'm sorry."

"Don't be." He cleared his throat. "I thought things would blow over with you if I pretended like it wasn't happening."

In his shoes, I probably would have done the same. I slipped my hand in his. "Not like you can control what I do." A genuine smile teased my lips. "Maybe now my friend can stop being something he's not."

"Right. A lot of good coming out of the closet has done me so far."

"Seth, you haven't given people a chance." I swung our arms. "You want people to be happy when you've spent forever pretending to be someone else. What did you expect?"

"Sometimes I can't believe how blind you are." He pulled away and walked to the ledge.

My heart picked up speed. Had he changed his mind about jumping?

"You think because you accept me, everyone else will. Remember the 'girl who didn't like boys?'"

I did. She'd been a pariah in high school—nameless other than her nickname. Shyness had kept me out of the limelight, ostracism her.

"Now I'm the boy who *did* like boys." He turned to me. "Rockin', right?"

"That was high school," I whispered without conviction.

"God! You're naïve!"

I hoped my inner wince didn't show. Still, Seth spoke the truth. The world was less than receptive to gays. Even so, I thought—hoped—things would be different for him. He'd always been the All-Star. The one everyone loved. Always found a way to fit in. As much as I wanted to deny the facts, being gay was anything but "normal" in our world.

Seth turned to the ledge and leaned over.

"Don't!" I screamed at the same time he yelled, "Hey!"

Seth glanced back at me and shook his head. Annoyance filled his face before he returned his attention over the ledge. "Come up to the roof and unlock the door."

A few seconds of silence passed before a guy called, "yeah sure. Give me a couple of minutes."

"We've got time. Not like we're going anywhere." Seth laughed, giving me a taste of the way things used to be. He faced me, all amusement gone. Seth—my actor friend.

"Sorry," I said though I wasn't sure for what. I just wanted peace... the good times we once had together.

"So am I." He pushed off the barrier. "You don't have to worry about me. I'm not going to do anything stupid."

I didn't believe him but remained silent.

Seth nodded to me. "What are you going to do with that?"

"With what?"

His eyes dipped to my side. "The letter."

I lifted my hand, Seth's note crushed in my fist. Proof my friend was not okay. The importance of reporting suicide attempts so people could get help entered my mind, but he seemed fine… better at least. Except, his problems still existed. We hadn't solved anything... not really. We were still estranged, and he was still gay.

Emotions hit me hard and fast. Tears momentarily blurred my vision with the relief I still had Seth… well, alive at least, and a bit of grief at losing him, losing the relationship we had.

"Alex?" Concern pitched his voice a little higher than normal.

In an instance, he had me wrapped in his arms. My entire body shook with sobs. I tried not to be embarrassed when a glob of snot flew out my nose to be reeled in by the next snort and hit me on the cheek.

I smeared it with the back of my hand and hoped nothing remained to dry to a shiny crust.

His hand rubbed slow circles between my shoulders which comforted me, but at the same time made it all worse. Like people giving their condolences at a graveside funeral.

"I'm sorry, Alex." Seth hugged me tighter. "I didn't mean to hurt you."

And he'd called me naïve. Jumping from the roof—how could he not think that would hurt me? Like kindle, a tiny spark of anger lit, my tears acting as fuel. I pushed at him, pounded my fist into his chest hard enough to jam my wrist. I clenched my teeth but a single word—"shit"—still squeezed past my lips.

"Feel better?" Seth rubbed his pectoral.

"No."

He chuckled.

I wished I had kicked his shin, because one thing for sure, the jab hurt me far more than it hurt him.

The door crept open, and I fumbled to wipe my face clean. Crying in front of Seth was one thing but in front of a stranger? Uhm no. These days, I didn't even let my parents see my tears.

"You okay up here?" a guy said.

"Yeah." Seth stepped around me. "I appreciate it, man."

"Sorry I took so long."

"No problem. I got it from here."

Seth and Mr. Stranger chatted it up while I turned invisible.

A switch flipped inside at being resigned to my former status—nothing but an extra to Seth's leading role. His fame or infamy, as it were now, wasn't a cause for jealousy, not at all. I just wanted something of my own... something beyond being an extension of my best friend. The role stifled me until the air was too thin to breathe. I had to get the heck out. And that was what I did, shoved past Seth and squeezed by the cutie blocking the door.

Sure I was upset, but I wasn't blind to dark hair which curled at his shoulders, nice full lips, big brown eyes. Bummer I was too shy to make a move and likely hideous with eyes surely puffy and red-rimmed.

"Hey, man, thanks," Seth said. "I guess we're in a hurry."

The stairs were a lot easier to descend. I saved time by hopping down the bottom four steps. My speed didn't keep me ahead of Seth as he pounded after me and jumped in front as I rounded the stairwell to the next set.

"Ease up, will ya?" He could have at least had the dignity to be winded.

I grabbed him by the arm to push him aside. He didn't move.

"Look, I'm not going to—" He looked over his shoulder. "I'm not going to you know what, okay?"

He didn't even get it, treated his attempted suicide like some big game for me to get over, as if missing him would mean nothing. Like it was okay for him to star in my life for the past twelve years then quit, just like that. No mess, except for the one he'd planned to leave for me as I walked to his dorm. Well, I didn't need that. "Screw you."

His eyes flinched as if I'd rammed my fingers at them. I darted around him, almost made it to the stairs. Seth snatched me from the edge and pressed me against the wall. One hand held me by the waist, his other hand slapped above my head. My heart fluttered as he leaned close, the scent of his mouthwash tickling my nose. I swallowed, wanting to lift to my toes and close the distance. Fear kept me immobilized.

"Is this what you want?" His voice deepened, adding a hint of sexiness. His lashes lowered, and I knew he was looking at my mouth.

I couldn't help but lick my lips and close my eyes. This was it, my turn to take my place next to Seth. To be to him what he needed.

"I don't love you like that, Alex."

My eyes popped open, met his sky blue ones. "What?"

"I never have... never will. You'll always be my friend, but nothing more."

Funny how tone of voice made all the difference in perception, because his minty breath turned harsh on my eyes, sending my lids into a convulsive flutter.

Who in the world took care of their dental hygiene before taking the final leap? And if he dared ask me about the tears smarting my eyes, I'd poke one of his so he'd know cruel words weren't the only things which made eyes water. I shoved him. "I know."

"Sometimes I'm not sure you do." Seth still towered over me, not the least bit moved by my push. After all we talked about on the roof, why was he doing this?

"May I go now?"

He stepped back.

I ducked under his arm and headed down stairs. "I was only trying to help *you*." *Sure you were, Alex.*

"Well, I don't need your help." His voice echoed in the stairwell, but at least he didn't follow.

I called back, "I need to study for Monday's test. I'll talk to you later."

For what test, I didn't know. But Seth didn't answer, and that was good enough for me. If I found the need to cry, I'd do it in the privacy of my own dorm... not on the steps with Seth toying with my emotions.

Chapter 15

♥

I rolled over for the umpteenth time. Images of Seth broken on the sidewalk kept me from sleeping and filled my dreams when I did. By the time the first rays of sunlight filtered into my room, I was zombified.

The radio switched on way too loud and startled me. Wide-eyed awake and my heart jack hammering to The Outsider by The Daylights, I glared at the clock which flicked seven oh one. I yanked the blankets to my ears before finally pounding the snooze button, not wanting to hear the song—a reminder of Seth's future.

A bit of irrational anger sparked at the idea my friend would ditch those who loved him—quietly, secretly—without any regards to their feelings.

A familiar sense of guilt hit, the emotion quickly becoming my new friend. Seth hurt, and I sulked about the effects his departure would have had on me. I couldn't help myself. He was my everything. *My everything*.

If I'd been with him instead of Dink, who meant little, Seth might not have ever considered suicide. I'd failed him. I'd abandoned him long before he'd tried to abandon me.

I threw off the covers. Within minutes I had my clothes on and was out the door. It took all my willpower not to race to his place like some eight-year-old straight off the school bus, but I managed. Fist pumping, I faked a power walk despite not dressing the part of exercise guru. Early morning fitness buffs, all about getting up early on a Saturday, smiled as I past. I arrived at Seth's room, huffing and regretting the fast pace I'd taken. After a breather and a swipe of my brow I knocked... and knocked, receiving no answer.

Worry sapped my remaining energy. Something had to give, and it wasn't me. I'd already put in all and come up short.

I took the elevator to the first floor, walked outside, and stood with no place to go. My stomach hiccupped at the thought of eating breakfast with stress drowning me in a sea of misery, while returning to bed and facing nightmares filled with a smashed Seth equaled fail.

I headed toward my dorm with far less determination than when I'd left. Halfway there, I stopped. I couldn't do this on my own, but my support was limited to Seth who was the problem, Dink whom I wanted to not know, and Trinity—my last hope... maybe. I detoured to her dorm.

♥

Having no reason to visit in the past, I'd never been inside Trinity's dorm, but the setup resembled Seth's. I found her room easily, but uncertainty kept me loitering outside her door.

What seemed like a good plan fifteen minutes ago seemed rash at eight thirty on a Saturday morning. Like Seth, she might not even be home. I stood—a moron—as folks stumbled around me in sleepwear, knocked on doors, and made plans for the day with their neighbors. What was I doing here?

I walked away as Trinity's door opened.

"Alex, come on in."

I turned to her standing at the threshold dressed in her normal preppy wear: khaki pants, a light blue blouse, and taupe loafers. Despite the day being beautiful and sunny, darkness prevailed inside her room with only a soft glow for lighting.

"Go on," she said as she headed down the hall. "I was just going to get a soda."

I hesitated only a moment before gratitude moved my feet inside the room.

Candles illuminated the living area and filled the room with a smoky lavender fragrance. Cozy, sure, but totally trampled all over the no fire regulation of the dorms. Leave it to Trinity to make her own rules.

Hoping she didn't mind, I flipped on the lights and walked to the African-style shelves decorating one corner of the room. The style resembled the Akye tribal art my mother loved so much: large pointed breasts and a small belly bump on a figure too slim to be realistic. I wondered if the piece had been custom made. The many arms with hands doubling as shelves were atypical of Akye or any African artwork I'd encountered on my shopping excursions with my mother. I traced the smooth dark wood, knowing the piece must have cost a fortune. Mom would do back flips to possess a treasure like that.

The top shelf featured a picture of a black couple who shared facial characteristics with Trinity. The man, sporting a shiny bald head, had an arm wrapped around a woman with shoulder length relaxed hair. On the shelf to the right, a young boy with close cropped hair wore a green jersey and knelt in front of a soccer ball. He resembled Trinity so much he had to be her brother.

Below his picture, a slightly younger Trinity stood with a white guy and two girls. I grinned, for the first time understanding her choice in wardrobe. The trio could have modeled for Prep USA.

The last picture, Trinity stood in front of four others who totally didn't fit her style. From left to right a smiling biker guy with short spiky black hair and dark eyeliner draped one arm around a girl with a matching black leather jacket. Her eyes crinkled at the corner as if holding back laughter. No doubt, his girlfriend. The same spiky hair graced her head, but her makeup was a bit more severe, add blood red lips. If that wasn't enough, she'd distinguished herself with an abundance of piercings... ears, nose, eyes. Who knew what she'd done below.

Then there was the stand in for Wednesday Addams—straight black hair to her waist, sad eyes, a corset top, and a long flowing black skirt. Without a doubt, her favorite store had to be Hot Topics. Where the other two went overboard with makeup, she wore none, making her ghostly and sorely in need of the sun.

Not quite part of the group, one guy stood to the side. He played GQ cover model in his all black attire, top three buttons undone, and platinum blond hair. His smile didn't reach his eyes which held a hint of disdain.

In front, Trinity wore her typical slacks and blouse, her mouth on the largest bong I'd ever seen.

Around the picture frame were the hand carved words:

If you call this anything other than a water pipe, I'll have to ask you to leave.

All those lunches together, and she'd never mentioned time spent with such an odd crowd. A group as peculiar as that would be worth talking about.

"I got you a cola," Trinity said from behind. "By the time I remembered to ask, I was already at the vending machines. Hope you don't mind."

"That works. Thanks."

Trinity passed it to me on her way to the futon, kicked her shoes off, and sat, curling her legs under. She patted the spot next to her. "Have a seat."

After my dash to Seth's and then her place, she didn't have to tell me twice.

She smiled. "You're my first visitor."

"No way!"

"Yes way!" she said, making me feel so high school.

I covered my embarrassment by cracking my can open and taking a sip. Trinity looked at me over hers, her eyes crinkling at the corners with amusement.

The soda fizzled down my throat as I gave one last swallow—all I could manage with the burning sensation. "So what's with the bong?"

Trinity's face went dead, her lips forming a straight line. "Please leave."

"What?" I stared at the picture of the four oddities plus one and a bong. My stomach did a little flip flop. *Was she serious?*

Trinity giggled and leaned back into a full laugh. Once my heart decided to pump blood back into my system I joined her.

She calmed a little, the grin on her face so wide she could try out for one of Joker's extras in a Batman movie. "In Washington they have shops that sell water pipes"—she fingered quotation marks in the air—"but bong is a drug term—drug paraphernalia. So the stores put up signs to pretend like they're not selling bongs for marijuana and crack. Stupid... I know." She laughed. "Like people are really going to use them for cigarettes. Oh, please."

I saw Trinity through new eyes. Perhaps the biker and emo crowd did suit her. After all, she'd played the instructor with her goodie-goodie exterior. Making the leap to drug addict wasn't too much of a stretch.

"That's not me," she said quickly. "I don't do drugs or anything like that. We bought it as a joke to commemorate my first time in one of those specialty shops. The water pipe-bong thing threw me too."

I believed her. Though, she could still be a functional druggie.

She laughed. "Enough about water pipes. What brings you to my humble abode?"

Once again, I debated the wisdom of coming. I hardly knew the gal, and already I wanted to dump my problems on her.

"Let me guess... a boy got you down?"

I sighed. "That obvious?"

I wanted to talk about Seth, but given the chance, I found I couldn't bring myself to spill my guts to a virtual stranger. It'd be like gossiping behind his back. My mind churned for a topic to save face and settled on the next biggest concern. "My boyfriend—"

"Wait! This calls for Poppycock." Trinity jumped to her feet and rushed to a cabinet in the mini-kitchen. A few open and slammed doors later and she returned with a giant bowl and a commercial bag labeled *Poppycock*. She poured out the contents—giant caramelized popcorn with some kind of nut—in the bowl she'd placed between us. "I love these things. Have some." She didn't wait for me before she popped one in her mouth. "Trust me. Poppycock takes the bitterness out of every situation."

I took a bite of a popcorn puff. An odd combination of crunchy and sugary goodness melted in my mouth. She was right. It was difficult to stay miserable while eating the delicious candied treat.

"Now tell me." Trinity took a few swallows of her soda between handfuls of Poppycock.

Where to begin? How about the end? "I've been dating this guy for a few weeks, and it's not working out. I just don't know how to... well—"

"Dump him?"

"Yeah."

"Try the 'it's not you, it's me' let-him-down-easy dumping." Trinity pursed her lips together but failed to hide the smile. And of course sealed lips couldn't keep the giggle down.

"Oh my gosh. For real?" *Please say you're joshing.*

She shrugged. "Not like you have a billion options. 'It's not working.' 'I'm dumping you.' 'It's over.' All comes down to the same thing. No matter how you put it, I doubt it'll be the highlight of his day."

Blunt... to the point... and so true. "I so hate you right now."

"Have some more Poppycock." She pushed the bowl toward me. "It'll cheer you up."

Chapter 16

♥

The woodpecker's insistent knocking continued for the third day in a row.

"Don't you worry it's trying to get at termites?" I asked my mother. *Tap, tap, tap.*

Mom's brows furrowed as she stirred the batter. "I don't think so. An inspector comes every year."

Tap, tap, tap. "Can't we do something? The bird's driving me crazy."

"Alex, are you in there?" my mother asked though her lips didn't move. "Alex."

Tap, tap, tap.

I jerked awake to the rapping. How long I'd been asleep, I couldn't tell, but night had fallen in the meantime. Trinity was right, poppycock had done the trick. I'd scarfed down enough to make me forget my worries, returned to my room, and finally managed to take a nap. Now, some inconsiderate dimwit wanted to ruin the little slice of sanity afforded to me.

I padded to the door and opened it to Dink heading down the hallway. "Hey."

He turned slowly, took me in from head to toe and back.

Lord knew how disheveled I looked. I ran a hand through my hair, well, at least until my fingers snagged within the tangles.

"We had a date, remember?" He returned and stopped so close, I was forced to crane my neck to meet his eyes.

I left the door open for him to follow if he wanted— or preferably not—and sat on the edge of my bed. "Sorry. A lot has been on my mind. I guess I forgot."

"Seth?" He hadn't moved from the threshold, instead, leaned against the doorjamb.

I tried to analyze his reluctance to enter but came up with nothing. "Yeah. Seth... and other things..."

"You wanna talk?" Dink. The guy had been so good to me over the last few weeks. He deserved better, yet I continued to use him like the twat I was.

"No."

"I understand." He pushed off the beam. "You probably want to be alone."

"Dink?"

He waited, letting silence fill our little piece of the world.

Speak. The words I needed to say bombarded me, but none of them seemed right. I sighed, nodded to the chair at my desk. "Do you want to sit?"

Dink twirled the chair around and straddled it. My itty bitty chair creaked under his weight as he leaned forward while I prayed it would hold.

"This isn't working." There. I'd said it. Just like ripping off a Band-Aid, except the guilt didn't fade, and I imagined I'd continued to feel like a heel long after Dink left.

He stared at me, his face expressionless, as if he hadn't heard a word. I opened my mouth to respond, but he cut me off with an "I see."

"It's not you—"

"It's me, right?"

"Yes... No!" I hopped from the bed and stood in front of him before falling to my knees, taking his hands between mine. Okay, maybe only held the tips of his sausage fingers. "It's me. It's me! It's never been about you."

He slipped from my grip, and the legs of the chair scraped the floor as he sat straight. "It's always been about Seth, right?"

"That's what I thought, too." I couldn't meet his eyes, nor did I want to sully my friend's reputation further by admitting he was suicidal, but the truth was, "Seth has his own problems, and I have issues which don't include him. I just didn't realize before."

The silence which greeted me was unbearable. I wanted to avoid the hurt, the anger, and overall unpleasantness I knew Dink wore on his face, but I couldn't stop myself from looking.

Dink did stoic well with the corner of his lips slightly angled downward—not quite a frown. His brows twitched once. Twice. Then his entire face drew into a scowl. "About time you came out and said it."

"What do you mean?" *Everyone had issues.*

He tilted back his head and laughed a sound as dry as the dust brushed from home plate. "I never had a chance. You were just toying with me, right? Like Seth with Cheyenne."

He stood, and I stumbled backward at his suddenness and landed on my butt. Being short was one thing, but having him tower over me while I sprawled on the floor was ridiculous. I scrambled out of his way as he stepped beyond me.

Dink stopped with his back to me. "You two belong together." He walked through the door and closed it with a click. In a way, his calm gesture was worse than if he'd slammed the door shut.

I couldn't be mad at Dink calling it like it was... saying exactly what had been going through my mind from the moment I'd agreed to date him.

I picked myself off the floor, grabbed my cell phone, and speed dialed one for Seth.

He answered on the first ring. "What's up?"

Just checking to see if you're still alive. "I hadn't heard from you today."

"I haven't heard from you either." His voice went into complete defense mode.

Everything in me said to fight back like I normally did. With our friendship so precarious, and possibly his state of mind also, I didn't want to push. "How are you doing?"

"If you're asking if I've reconsidered leaping, the answer's no. Last night was a once in a lifetime opportunity."

"You can't blame me for being worried, Seth."

"Don't be."

I laughed. "Telling me not to worry is not going to stop me from worrying?"

"Think about it." Seth's heavy sigh came through the phone. "Do you really think I would have answered if I'd planned... well, I wouldn't have answered the phone, okay?"

"I guess."

"I'm dropping out."

"What?" It was one of those moments where I'd heard, but my mind struggled to understand. So even as Seth repeated himself, I wanted to tell him, *I know. I heard you the first time.*

"What about..." I wanted to say baseball, but according to him, his sports career was over. My lame brain scrambled to finish the question. "...school?"

"I can't deal with school right now. Maybe next quarter... or semester..."

Or next year... or never. One stumble and my BFF decided to throw his future away.

"Seth. How about I come over? We can talk."

"I'm kind of tired right now. I'll talk to you tomorrow."

Void filled the earpiece—the kind of dead space when the connection's been lost.

"Seth?" I said into the emptiness. The inconceivable had happened, driving another wedge into our friendship. I stared at the cell before returning it to my ear. "Seth?"

I hit the end button—as if it mattered—placed my phone on the dresser, and peeled off my clothes. As long as I had a sleepless night ahead of me, I should at least be comfortable.

With the lights off and me in bed, I stared at the dark ceiling, wondering if my world would ever be right again.

Chapter 17

♥

Football practice started at the break of dawn. I didn't belong in the bleachers watching the guys crash into one another—an imitation of the collisions in my life. The alternative, lying in bed while thoughts of Seth tortured me, offered no better solution. All the reasons he should stay in college with me weren't good enough, not when a fresh start waited for him at another university. A new beginning with endless possibilities.

Like Van Buren. *Here* was supposed to be his opportunity to be the person he wanted to be. A place where he didn't need to hide like in high school. Yet he'd repeated the mistake like a bad rerun. When would he allow himself to be his own person?

His own person. My own person, free of Seth's shadow. I'd turned into a shadow of myself, accepted the role readily. What happened to the little girl who'd existed before Seth? The little girl who'd stood up for herself... and sometimes for others too. I hadn't been a sidekick back then. I'd been just... me. Shy, yes, but me, nonetheless.

I wanted to be that little girl again, but I'd been Seth's sidekick for so long, I wasn't sure I could find her. Even now I lived in a shadow of a world, hiding in the bleachers, stalking the ex-boyfriend I'd dumped, and spying on the boy my BFF loved. How pitiful was that?

The coach yelled for the team to get a drink. Dink broke away from the rest of the group and headed straight toward me. I wanted to run, but that was sillier than doing the emo creeper thing. I hopped down the bleachers to meet him instead. Perhaps we'd avoid a scene if we kept our voices low. I'd seen enough lovers' spats in high school to know I didn't want the experience as an adult in college.

I waited on the bottom step, wanting a little more height for the confrontation. When Dink stopped in front of me, I still wasn't eye to eye with him.

"Hi." It was hard to believe that weak whisper came from me.

Dink pulled off his helmet, revealing a damp mop of strawberry blond hair. He swiped aside a few strands plastered to his forehead. "What are you doing here?"

"I don't know." *Lame. Lame. Lame.* One hundred percent accurate, but still lame. Saying I'd gotten lost would have been better.

"Right." He glanced over his shoulder at the other guys taking turns at the water cooler.

"You were right."

He turned back to me. "What?"

"I said you were right. What I did was no better than what Seth did to Cheyenne, and I'm sorry."

He frowned, but I couldn't tell what it meant. "Yeah. Okay."

Apology accepted?

He looked at the team again. If he was so anxious, he should have stayed with his buddies. Besides, the coach would be calling them at any moment. *No rest for the weary* was his motto.

"I just figured we'd pass each other on campus from time to time." I shrugged, hoping I pulled off innocent. "Maybe we can avoid the dirty looks and all."

This time Dink pursed his lips along with the frown.

"Or not," I said.

"Wrap it up, ladies," the coach called through the bullhorn.

"We'll see. I gotta go." Dink didn't wait for a response as he jogged onto the field.

I sat where I stood. Talking to Dink was easier and harder than I'd imagined. No yelling. No personal blows. Admitting to my wrong had never felt so right, yet left me strangely unfulfilled. The limbo of *we'll see* was far from the closure I'd hoped to receive, but I supposed it was better than nothing.

I wanted to stay and let the clatter of football uniforms console me, but knowing Dink and Bruce were in the mix was less than comforting. I stood, stretched, and headed to the campus cafe for an early breakfast. As much as I wanted to stop by Seth's dorm, I couldn't brave another rejection. It was one thing for him to hang up on me, quite another to have the door slam in my face, or worse—Seth turn and walk away forever.

♥

Hungry children scavenge the dumps in Nicaragua to get a decent meal on the table for their family, my mother would say after I'd left too much food on my plate. *Those kids work in the dry dust with the sun beating down so hard the heat rolls off the dirt in waves. You think your steak would have gone wasted?*

Mom knew how to lay on the guilt. If I'd known she'd mentally accompany me to breakfast, I'd never had come. My appetite was crap with Seth and Dink's faces floating in my mind's eye. All but my toast ended up in the trash as I headed out the cafeteria.

"Alex!"

I froze in place to a voice I'd never forget. The voice I wanted to hear above anything. The voice I dreaded hearing—Seth.

"Hello?" someone said behind me. "Can we keep moving?"

I remembered to walk forward, unblocking the doorway.

"Thanks." That someone bumped past.

Seth jogged to me, helmet in hand. I tried to meet his eyes, but his wandering gaze made that impossible. I'd turned invisible to the one person who saw me better than anyone.

Silence befell us and stretched into the most awkward I'd ever experienced. I wanted to end it but feared if I spoke, my moment with my BFF would be over, and he'd disappear into the void.

"I talked to the dean." Seth looked beyond me, shuffling from foot to foot. "I'm leaving today."

My heart stopped. The constant beat which had been my steady companion since birth was gone, leaving an emptiness. I wanted to breathe, but it didn't matter anymore. Just like that, the break in the quiet had stolen my friend.

He focused glossy eyes on me. "I stopped by your dorm."

My mind supplied the response. Like an automaton, my mouth answered, "I went to the field to watch the football practice."

Seth's lips thinned to a tight line, and his brows knotted in the center before he responded with a simple "oh."

I sighed. *Get over it, Alex. No sense acting surprised over something you knew would happen. Be the friend you've always been.* "Where are you going?"

"Home."

Home. The same place I'd go if I needed to reboot. If anything, Seth deserved a break. "Are you going to tell your father?"

"I don't know."

Out of words, I chewed the inside of my cheek. Then a thought occurred to me. "Do they even know you're coming?"

"Not yet." Seth gave a rare lopsided grin. The kind that said he was out of his element and clueless of what to do next. He couldn't maintain it long, and it fell leaving a frown.

I wanted to hug him, tell him it was okay and everything would work out, but honestly, I wasn't sure. My friend dropped out of school because he'd been forced out of the closet. The only thing for certain was, "your dad loves you regardless."

"Yeah." His voice deepened.

"You should have told him long ago."

Seth looked away and kicked a pebble.

"I hope you'll come back," I said.

He cleared his throat. "I doubt that'll happen."

"Well... call me when you get home."

Again, one corner of Seth's mouth lifted in a semblance of a smile, though he didn't quite manage the happy effect. "You know I will."

Silence took over our conversation as we stared at one another. My friend—leaving to escape the truth, as if running away would change who he was inside. Me—left behind to rediscover myself all over again—to be the forefront of my life rather than a shadow of his.

The heaviness of the situation compressed me, but in a strange way I felt liberated. I could float away with the freedom. An odd mixture—like a fever which left the skin hot but the flesh beneath chilled.

I was more than Seth's friend. I was me—Alexandria Carmichael, aka Alex. People noticed me even when I tried to remain hidden behind my friend's stature.

"Well, I guess this is it." Seth lifted his eyes to me, displaying a shyness I'd never known from him.

I closed the distance, wrapped my arms around him. He didn't hesitate to return a tight squeeze. This was what I remembered; this was what I missed—the closeness. I didn't want to release him, but I did, and it was as if the moment was gone forever.

"Okay." He looked everywhere but at me. I didn't blame him. I couldn't take my eyes off him, wanted to commemorate the moment, but if he returned my stare, I'd have to break eye contact. We'd reached a point only one of us could immortalize, and I was glad it was me.

He walked away without another word, which was a relief. I hated goodbyes, they seemed so final.

"Don't forget to call when you arrive," I yelled.

He lifted his helmet, but didn't turn back, didn't answer. Just as well, it made pretending he was going home for a short break easier... like in high school when he went to football camp. A few weeks later, he'd be back... except this time he wouldn't.

My eyes ached, and I let them rather than allowing the tears to fall. I'd done enough crying these days. Each time had left me physically exhausted. With my next class in less than a half an hour, I didn't have time to be tired; I barely had time to grab my books from my room first. I headed to my dorm, focusing on how to avoid the emotions twirling inside.

Chapter 18

♥

Trinity gave me a pitying look before she set her tray on the table and slid into the booth. "You've been acting weird today. Want to talk?"

"Not really." I pushed a tomato with my fork, letting it tumble down my salad and into a pool of ranch dressing.

"You might feel better if you let it out."

Let it out? If my eyes lost any more moisture, they'd shrivel into raisins and fall out my head.

Her brows drew together as if God put them on her face for the sole purpose of showing sympathy. "Anything I can do?"

"I—" *I what?* The words stalled on the tip of my tongue. Where to start: Dink or Seth? The two situations were so intertwined, they were impossible to unravel.

Trinity lowered her lashes and twirled a French fry in ketchup. "I don't want to pry. I'll listen if you ever need an ear."

And just like that, my opportunity to share faded until next time. "Thanks."

"No problem." Her eyes met mine. "I just know how tough being alone is sometimes."

Her gaze flicked past me, a frown forming on her face. I wanted so much to see who or what approached but managed to prevent myself from twisting in my seat like a nosy bumpkin even when Trinity's right eyebrow lifted.

"Hey." Dink stopped in front of our table. His gaze lingered on Trinity before settling on me.

My heart hiccupped, and I prayed an ugly scene wasn't about to unfold.

He rested a hand on the table. "About earlier..."

Yeah? I took a deep breath and held it. He probably wanted me to fill in the silence, but I'd already had my say... offered my apologies.

He glanced at Trinity again before squatting to my level and lowering his voice. "I wanted to tell you, no hard feelings. I could tell you weren't interested long before I tried." He gave a chuckle lacking in humor. "Can't help a guy for wanting a challenge, right?"

He considered me a challenge? The corner of my lip lifted at the subtle compliment, and his smile turned genuine.

"So we're good?" he asked.

"I hope so."

He stood, breaking the connection. "We're having a party tonight at the Alpha House. Stop by. Bring a friend."

I exchanged glances with Trinity, and her eyes widened, silently urging me to say yes. For her sake, I said, "I'll think about it."

"Great. Nine o'clock." He smiled at Trinity before walking away.

"Was that Dink?" she asked.

"Yeah."

"Did you two have a blow out?"

"Something like that."

"Oh." Trinity pursed her lips, hitting me with a long hard look. "Did he pull something funny?"

I cringed at her accusation toward the one person innocent of blame. "Not exactly."

"No?" She leaned forward, and her eyes took on a wicked gleam. "Spill it."

"I took your advice." I couldn't tear myself away from the intensity of her stare which had the power to pull information straight through my forehead. "Breakups are just hard, you know?"

One of her eyebrows rose in thoughtfulness before she settled deep in her seat. "I see."

I totally felt like she did see... right through me. I'd said little, but it was as if I'd already bared my soul, liberating me of a burden. "I thought he'd help me take my mind off my best friend. Seth. He's gay... my best friend."

I waited for the judgment to come.

The widening of her eyes was noticeable but negligible and overshadowed by a growing smile full of acceptance. "Well, go on."

That was all the encouragement I needed. My mouth and tongue moved like they had a will of their own, spilling the story of my not-so-secret love obsession for my BFF, his for Bruce, my unsuccessful attempt to substitute Dink for Seth, and Seth's attempted suicide followed by his escape from college.

Trinity took it all in, asking clarifying questions and adding a few winces. With the wackiness of the situation, I didn't blame her though.

She sat back. "So what you're saying is Dink is a free agent."

"What?" I laughed.

"As in available."

I chuckled a little more, but Trinity didn't even crack a smile. I sobered as I realized she was one hundred percent serious. "You're interested in Dink?"

"Well?"

I tried to muster an ounce of jealousy over Trinity scoping out my newly estranged boyfriend, but images of him shoveling food into his mouth like a garbage truck invaded my thoughts. Trinity wanted Dink? Who was I to scrap over something so trivial? I shrugged. "He's up for grabs if you're interested."

Her lips quivered, amusement twinkling in her eyes. Trinity shook her head, doing the Kool-Aid man proud with her grin. "I'm not. He'd crush me."

Dink's beefy paws engulfing my hands came to mind before I pictured her—a couple of inches shorter than me—with him. My laughter bubbled over then Trinity joined me until tears streaked her face.

She sobered a bit. "I don't know why I asked. I guess I was just curious about how severe your attachment"—she fingered quotation marks—"issues were."

Attachment issues. Yeah, that summed it up. I wanted to pretend the heart chose whom to love, and I had no choice, but the truth of the matter was I never should have entertained romantic ideas about Seth. He hadn't even been able to count on me when he needed because I'd tried to push beyond the friendship. Now it was too late. He was gone, dealing with the mess the best he could, while I remained, trying to move on as the gap between us grew larger.

Trinity had that thoughtful look again as she studied me. She was even more of a people watcher than I was.

"So you want to go to the party tonight?" I asked.

She cocked her head to the side. "Do you?"

"No," was my immediate answer. Partying had never been my style, but I also didn't want to be Hermit Girl. Seth would have dragged me—my link to the outside world. "But I don't want to closet myself in my dorm room."

"Yeah. The same old scene is starting to make me a little claustrophobic these days."

I leaned forward. I almost felt conspiratorial as I whispered, "I think we should go."

Trinity's eyes gleamed with excitement. "So do I."

"Fine! We'll do it." I took a bite of my salad and munched. For the first time in forever, I felt like my own person... capable of enjoying life without Seth as my guide.

Chapter 19

♥

My earlier bravado faded as I watched students enter and leave Alpha Epsilon. Trinity linked her arm with mine. She was big into that for some reason. Fine by me, it gave me a sense of camaraderie, and I needed the extra boost for the next move: entering the lion's den.

"This is it." She didn't give me an opportunity to respond before she moved forward, giggling as she pulled me along.

My foot landed on the bottom step just as Bruce appeared in the doorway. I froze where I stood despite the tug Trinity gave me.

"Hey, Sam." Bruce tapped the guy at the door on the shoulder. "Whoever was on ice duty screwed up. We're going to need more than two—" He focused on me, his lips still rounded from his last word. His mouth moved wordlessly before he flicked his gaze to Trinity then to me again. His head turned to Sam, but his eyes remained on me as he finished, "—two bags. Think you can handle a run. I'll man the door while you're gone."

"Yeah, sure. I could use the break." Sam focused on me the entire time he descended the stairs. I didn't recognize him, but from the attention he gave me, no doubt he'd heard all sorts of bad news from his frat brothers, Dink and Bruce, and likely had seen the Seth incident at Rush first hand.

"I don't think I want to do this." I backed away, only to be held in place by Trinity.

She leaned close to my ear. "We're doing this. You can't hide forever. What are you going to do? Run away like your friend, Seth?"

I couldn't do that. My entire future rested on finishing college, finding a job, living happily ever after.

"If you back down now, you'll be looking over your shoulder 'til the day you leave this place. Is that what you want?"

Bruce hadn't moved from his post, his expression unreadable. Then again, why should he? He was on his turf, and I was the invader. At that moment, I'd give anything to read his mind. Did he want to hurt me like he'd hurt my friend?

"You've done nothing wrong." Trinity chuckled. "Other than leading Dink on, that is, and he's so over the break up."

Sure he let my slight go, but it didn't make what I did okay. "I don't belong here."

Trinity nudged me forward. "Take back your life."

Take back your life—the first thing she'd said which resonated with me. I wanted my life back. Above all, I wanted to be independent... my own person. Something other than a shadow. I climbed the stairs until I stood face to face to Bruce.

He could have stared down his nose at me. My connection to Seth warranted no less. Yet he bent his head to look me fully in the eyes, as if I deserved at least that much respect. His gaze was full of apprehension while lacking the animosity I'd expected and left me at a loss for words.

Take back your life. Trinity's voice echoed in my head as if she'd spoken them aloud.

I wanted to, though I wasn't sure how to obtain it. *Baby steps*, I told myself. "Hi."

"I didn't expect you here. I heard you and Dink broke up." Bruce's monotone voice put me on high alert. I couldn't tell if he was controlling his anger, giving me a fresh start, or what. At least he wasn't yelling.

"We did." My voice shook, and I swallowed before continuing. "Dink invited me."

"Oh?" Bruce stood a little taller and crossed his arms. "He didn't mention inviting..." His brows lifted slightly. "...guests."

Of course not. Who invites an ex-girlfriend to a party the day after breaking up? "I'll leave." I backed away but bumped into Trinity.

Bruce's posture relaxed, and he gave a heavy sigh. "Wait."

"Excuse me?"

"You can stay." He turned sideways, giving me room to pass.

"You sure?"

"Yeah. If Dink wants you here, I'm not going to stand in his way. I don't own Alpha Epsilon."

In other words, *you can enter, but I don't want you here.* I couldn't help but take his unsaid words one step further: I could stay on campus, but if I left, even better. For some reason, that stoked me. I had as much right as any student to experience an enjoyable life at Van Buren. I earned my place with good grades and too many extra-curricular activities.

Trinity was right. I wasn't to blame for Seth keeping his sexuality secret then coming out in the most unbecoming way.

"Seth has been my best friend since first grade," I started. "You of all people—a member of one of the tightest knit fraternities on campus—should know a little something about loyalty."

Bruce flinched.

I continued, "Yeah. I knew he was gay, but who was I to tell the world? And I certainly didn't make him come on to you." I gave a half laugh. "Go ahead. Hate me for standing by my friend, but you know what? I'd do it all over again. And if you're worthy at all of living in this frat house, you would have stood by any of your frat brothers also."

"Not if he were g—"

"Really? 'Honor and Loyalty, Always.'" I threw the slogan from the Alpha Epsilon brochure at him. "So now it's not always? Only sometimes?"

Bruce diverted his eyes.

With all that happened over the past few days, I was beyond tallying points. Instead, I lengthened my spine and held out a hand. "Truce?"

He stared at me so long, I almost pulled away, but then he reached out and warmed my palm with his. "Just promise you won't leave me in the dark next time one of your gay friends has a thing for me."

I let loose a few chuckles before I realized he hadn't joined me, his face dead serious. I sobered immediately and gave him a firm shake. "Deal."

"Thanks." He released me, nodded inside. "Dink has kitchen duty. All the way to the back and through the swinging doors."

Trinity, arm still linked with mine, huddled close and whispered, "you're doing great."

Right. Tell that to my sweaty back. At least I'd overcome one hurdle. One more piece of my life wrestled back into place. My legs wanted to bounce me along. Only Trinity holding me down kept me from doing so.

"Birds of a flock," Cheyenne's voice came from the right and full of venom.

I looked in her direction as she drew closer. My high flittered away, leaving me grounded.

She snapped her gum between her teeth as she came to stand in front of me, one hip cocked to the side with a hand landing on top. Her lips puckered in a funky smile, and her eyebrows twitched as she looked from me to Trinity and back again. "Why am I not surprised? It would make sense the faggots would stick together."

Trinity's proximity suddenly felt less conspiratorial and a whole lot of questionable. My temperature rose to the point my skin prickled with the emergence of fresh sweat.

I finally understood the reason Seth guarded his secret so closely. I wasn't gay but couldn't help the shame associated with being accused—like getting caught doing something criminal.

In an instant, Cheyenne had turned me into a pariah... the girl who didn't like boys. My little corner of the wall beckoned me to return to invisibility.

Trinity released me, sauntered to the cheerleader.

Cheyenne held a vindictive grin as she smacked away at her gum, towering over my alleged lover.

A crooked smile bordering on seductive crept onto my newfound friend's face before she slid her hand up Cheyenne's side, to her breast, and around to her back.

Cheyenne didn't move an inch. Only her eyes, growing wider by the milliseconds, showed any acknowledgement. Trinity wet her lips with her tongue before rising to her tippy toes and pulling Cheyenne's head down. Cheyenne offered little resistance when Trinity's lips pressed against hers. The kiss was so deep, my eyelids fluttered in convulsions as Cheyenne stumbled backward.

"Yeah. You're right." Trinity wiped her mouth before swatting Cheyenne on the butt and stepping away. "Us queers do need to stick together."

All eyes zeroed on Cheyenne as she stood in the center of the room... alone. Years ago, Seth and I had lost track of time at a water park. By the time we decided to leave, Seth was red and queasy from the sun. The look on Cheyenne's face reminded me of the long ago moment.

"I'm not—" Cheyenne search the faces around the room. "I'm not—"

"How many times do I have to tell you? I hate cherry flavor." Trinity pulled a wad of gum from her mouth and flicked the mass which nailed the cheerleader solid between the brows.

Cheyenne's face screwed into a grimace as she scraped her fingers across her forehead and stared at the chewed gob. She shook it free with a "ugh," her mouth dangling open.

Whispers circulated around the room to the tune of "I didn't know she was gay." "Neither did I." "I'm not surprised... hiding under the cover of bitch-hood."

Cheyenne blinked a few times, her eyes growing shinier with each flicker. Her breath hitched once. Twice. Then she turned and pushed her way through the gathered crowd.

As students closed behind her, one by one, pairs of eyes landed on Trinity and me. At that moment, I wanted nothing more than to crawl under the nearest table. Or perhaps follow Cheyenne out the door and run to my dorm.

"Hey." Trinity shrugged. "It takes all kinds to make the world go round, right?"

Silence.

I had to hand it to Trinity, she held her ground regardless. One by one, acceptance filled faces, and the group dispersed as if they hadn't just witnessed the biggest spectacle since Bruce tried to thrash Seth for the very same thing a few weeks ago.

I turned to Trinity. "Why did you do that?"

She scowled. *You can't be that stupid*, the frown said. "One—some people don't stop until you put them in place. Two—I had a feeling you'd had enough of her. Three—I didn't think you'd do it for yourself."

The way she said the last had me shrinking in shame.

"Don't worry." She interlocked her arm with mine again. "We'll take care of each other. I've got your back, and you've got mine, right?"

The same way it should have been between Seth and me. I didn't want a replacement best friend. The one I had was perfectly good enough if he'd only overcome the blow to his social rep.

"I'm not trying to replace your friend," Trinity said like she had a link inside my mind. "I'm just saying a gal can and *should* have more than one friend, if you know what I mean."

Her words hurt. Not because what she said was mean, but rather she'd verbalized something I'd withheld from myself. I'd been so busy trying to patch up the fragile relationship with Seth that I hadn't realized what was wrong with it in the first place. I'd isolated myself, thinking he was enough for me. He wasn't. In fact, even adding Trinity to the mix wasn't enough. Whether I had one friend or a gazillion, I had to be enough for myself. So the big question: Was I?

Chapter 20

♥

"Dink's waiting in the kitchen." I skirted the throng of people.

Trinity said nothing, leaving me alone to my thoughts. As talkative and straight forward as she was, she still seemed to know when to keep her mouth shut. A trait I appreciated.

I pushed open the swinging doors and walked into chaos. The snacks and drinks scattered about the kitchen made a myriad of colors which would put Thomas Kincaid to shame. On the island counter, a two-liter bottle fizzled onto the floor and splattered the fridge with a wash of orange. Dink stood over the sink, ripping paper towels off the rack hand over fist. Poor guy. So flustered, he lacked the common sense to contain the mess before cleanup. I set the soda upright, soiling my hand as foam volcanoed over the rim with one last spurt.

Dink spun around, covered in soda and holding enough paper towels to make the Brawny Lumberjack beat him senseless with his own wad.

Trinity chuckled behind me.

I shook a bit of moisture from my hand. "Problem?"

An unbecoming shade of orange and red mottled Dink's face as his lips worked wordlessly. At a time like this that dimpled smile of his would have come in handy.

I rounded the counter and ripped a few paper towels from my human rack. "Looks like you could use a little help."

"Yeah." His shoulders slumped as he glanced over my head to where Trinity stood. *Did he have a thing for her?*

His invitation to the rush party came back to me. Not a direct request but one to Seth which had included me. I pitied the guy with his round about ways for accomplishing his goals. Then again, I understood the fear of rejection.

I tore a few more paper towels off Dink. "I'm going to need these."

"Thanks," he said as I turned to the counter and blotted the mess.

I raised my brows at Trinity and gave a pointed nod toward Dink.

"I'll help also." She rushed forward, grabbed the remaining paper towels from Dink, and set to work on the floor.

"Coming through," a voice outside the kitchen yelled. Trinity tumbled backward, barely avoided the door swinging toward her face as a guy burst in.

"Need more chips." The guy—Bill—looked around the kitchen. His gaze landed on me, then Trinity before fixating on Dink with a frown. "Uh…" His eyes resumed the search, raking over the cluttered counters. He grabbed a random bag—"got it"—and left.

People came; people went as I worked alongside Trinity and Dink. A comfortable silence befell us, not unlike my quiet moments with Seth. For the next half hour we weaved amongst one another, reorganizing the room until all we had left to do was sit and relax.

"I wish you two had been here when the goods first arrived," Dink said.

"I guess all it needed was a woman's touch." I bumped shoulders with Trinity as we shared a laugh.

"Yeah." Dink gave a half smile before letting it fade. He glanced to Trinity then back to me. "No hard feelings."

Oh lord. Please don't make a tacky move on Trinity while I'm sitting here. Wrong time, Dink. Wrong time. I refused to look at Trinity, mentally urging her to make herself scarce and save us all the embarrassment. Instead, she settled deeper in her seat.

"What I'm thinking..." His eyes shifted to Trinity again. "If you all want to hang out or come to some of the games, I'm cool with that."

"Dink." I said his name to give me time to think. I could already feel myself being shoved into the corner role of sidekick. I refused to go peacefully this time. "You don't have to go through me to get to Trinity."

His face blotted that awful myriad of red undertones as his eyes darted back and forth between Trinity and me. "I... I know."

"I'm actually not on the market." Trinity gave a soft and stress-free smile.

"Oh." Dink's gaze landed everywhere but on us.

"No hard feelings, right?" Trinity used his line against him.

"Right." Dink stood and made himself busy straightening a bag of pretzels. "The offer still stands. As friends, you know?"

"Of course," I said, not believing the transition from couple to friend would be so easy. Changing the dynamics of my relationship with Seth certainly hadn't been, but I was willing to try with Dink. Strike that. I *wanted* to give him a try. Though Dink wasn't my type in the sexual attraction department, he'd been decent to me. Like Trinity said, having a few extra friends didn't hurt.

I smiled. I was making friends... friends without Seth. A spot in my chest ached with happiness. I was going to get through this and be okay.

My cell phone rang, and I fumbled to pull it out of my back pocket. A quick check on the ID revealed Seth's number, sending my heart into a pitter-patter. "Hello?"

"Hey," he said. "Wanted to let you know I made it back home."

For the longest time Seth was home to me. If I returned to my parents' house, would that be home now? "Well?"

"Better than I'd expected. Mom ranted a bit. Dad sat quietly. You know how he is."

"Yeah."

"I told them I was... gay."

Tired of dealing with the questioning pseudo-sign language from Trinity and Dink, I walked to a corner, giving them my back. "And?"

"It set off an argument." He gave a dry laugh.

Anger burned inside of me that his parents would turn against him. "I can't believe it! Your da—"

"About who knew first."

My anger fizzled like embers being doused with water. "What?"

"They'd been speculating for a few years now." He laughed again, this time with more humor. "They'd been waiting for me to come out."

I wanted to be happy, but the suddenness of the situation left me confused. "That's good, right?"

"I guess."

The kitchen door opened, linking me back to the party as someone entered and left.

"What's up with the noise in the background?" Seth asked.

"I'm at an Alpha Epsilon party."

"Oh."

"Dink invited me."

"Hmm."

His simple response turned me into a Judas, though I hadn't betrayed him. I'd stood up to Bruce and won, and I refused to defend my actions now. Seth had left me friendless. What did he expect? I deserved to have relationships as much as anyone.

"Seth!" his mother called in the background. "Dinner time."

"I guess you've got to go," I said.

"Yeah."

I didn't want to hang up and instead let the silence fill the gap.

"Sorry I crapped out on you, Alex."

His apology was like a boulder being rolled off me. I could almost see us returning to the way things were... almost, but not quite.

"I guess I pulled a fast one on you," I said. *It was my fault the relationship changed*, I wanted to add.

"Yeah."

With nothing to say, the awkward silence returned. So odd to be having those with my BFF.

"Seth! Set the table," his mother called.

"I gotta go," Seth said.

I smiled, remembering dinner at his house, and his mother's annoyance with cold food. "Later."

"Yeah. Later."

The phone went dead. I hit end and returned the cell to my pocket. "That was Seth."

"We gathered," Trinity said.

"He came out to his parents."

Dink stiffened.

I tried not to let his fake "as long as it doesn't affect me" attitude rake me into irritation with little success. "You seemed to think Seth was a pretty decent guy before. You *and* Bruce. How many times did you two try to recruit him into your fraternity? Before he was eligible even. 'Join the football team,' you said! 'We'll put in a good word for you.' Remember?"

Dink's brows puckered, and he even had the nerve to clench his teeth, twitching jaws and all.

"Seth didn't change." I was on a roll. "Just your perception of him..." my voice trailed to a whisper as I thought how mine had too.

"About time someone came out and said the truth of the matter." Trinity crossed her arms. "No one should have to suffer for being gay." She speared Dink with a penetrating stare. "I can't believe what dicks some people can be."

Fire flashed in Dink's starburst eyes before he turned to an empty corner.

"Thank you, Trinity," I said. "Your support means a lot to me. Too bad you didn't get a chance to meet Seth. He could have used a friend like you."

Trinity didn't divert her pointed glare toward Dink. "Like I said, we can all use friends."

If I could turn back time and reclaim my old friendship with Seth, I would... stop myself before I twisted the love for him into something he didn't want. Too late for that; the damage was irreparable. Still, I couldn't help but see the good.

The invisible rift Seth had with his parents had closed, or at the very least was closing. My friend had the opportunity to start anew and be true to himself.

And me? I looked at Trinity—small but full of confidence—and hoped some of her attitude would rub off on me. Defending Seth was a step in the right direction. It felt good not to retreat for once.

"Well, you've made your feelings clear." Dink brushed past me and swung the kitchen door open, letting in the commotion. "I tried to compromise with you, but the gay wagon is not my thing."

With everyone speaking their mind, the façade was over. Strangely enough, I couldn't care less. Strike that—the truth freed me.

I smiled at Trinity and held out my hand. "Shall we?"

She laughed. "Of course."

This time when she came in reach, I linked my arm within hers, taking the lead. Head held high, I walked out of Alpha Epsilon, ready to start down a path as my own person instead of an extension of another.

"Gretel's?" I asked. "It's open all night on the weekends."

"Uh... How about Jacky's Place?" Trinity's eyes lit with excitement. "We have just enough time to make it. Plus, I know the owner."

"Sounds like a plan." *A new place for a new beginning.*

My phone rang, and I answered.

"Oh, by the way," Seth said from the other end. "Mom said you're having Thanksgiving with us."

I laughed. "I don't think my parents will approve of me ditching them on my mother's favorite holiday."

"Mom's arranged it all. Everyone's coming here. 'Family is what you make of it,' she said."

My eyes got a bit misty. *Family.* Ups or downs, Seth was an intricate part of mine, and he recognized it too.

"Of course." I let the facts wash over me. I should have been elated, but I wasn't. My relationship with Seth had downgraded from best friend to something else.

He'd once told me he didn't always like his little sister, but he always loved her. Not having siblings, I'd never understood what he'd meant before now.

I tried not to let the boulder crush me again. No matter how hard I clung to the past, the present kept pushing me forward. Though my heart was breaking, I forced myself to accept our relationship would never be the same, but we'd always be family. "Just remember, I loved you first."

"And now you love Dink." Bitterness crept into Seth's voice.

I looked at the frat house, full of students with their fickle likes and dislikes, Dink hidden amongst them. "No." Though I didn't move, I felt a little taller despite my short stature. "Now I love me too."

I'd said it, and the strangest thing; I believed every word.

Seth chuckle. "What's not to love?" If Seth had been by my side, he would have jabbed me in the shoulder. "Okay. I gots to go for real this time."

"Fine."

"Talk to you tomorrow."

I smiled. "Of course."

I turned to Trinity as I put my phone away.

"We good?" she asked.

I shrugged. "If not good, better."

Trinity penetrated me with that stare which left me exposed then smiled. "Yeah. You'll be fine. I get the feeling you're the bouncy type."

I cringed as bubbly cheerleader came to mind. "Bouncy type?"

"The type who springs back, girl." Her eyebrows crinkled. "Overcomes trials?"

Emotions scrubbed raw, I'd run out of salve long ago. My mouth lifted in a half grin. "Survivor is more like it."

"Like I said, you'll be fine."

I didn't know her like I knew Seth, but strangely enough, I believed her. Not because of what she said, but because I believed in myself... for once. "We better get going before that place closes."

"Jacky's Place."

"Right, Jacky's Place."

She took my hand and dragged me toward her car. Whether or not a friendship with her lasted, didn't matter. That I'd made a start and broken out of the old me was enough.

If you enjoyed *I Loved You First*. Please support the author by reviewing this work at Amazon, Goodreads, Barnes & Nobles, or Smashwords. Thank you.

About the author:

Reena Jacobs is just your typical writer who loves to see her words in print. As an avid reader, she's known to hoard books and begs her husband regularly for "just one more purchase." Her home life is filled with days chasing her preschooler and nights harassing her husband. Between it all, she squeezes in time for writing and growling at the dog.

Connect with Reena online:

Email: reenajacobs@reenajacobs.com
Website: http://www.reenajacobs.com
Blog: http://www.reenajacobs.com/blog

Afterwards

One thing I've never understood is the animosity toward the LGBT community. I was raised in a Christian household.

Before any one gets ideas – I'm not a defect. I believe everything in the bible, but admit I don't understand it all and don't know how everything fits together. Still, I have no doubt of the validity of the Word.

How do I reconcile my Christian faith with my support of the LGBT community? The answer is simple, really.

> [34] Hearing that Jesus had silenced the Sadducees, the Pharisees got together. [35] One of them, an expert in the law, tested him with this question: [36] "Teacher, which is the greatest commandment in the Law?"
>
> [37] Jesus replied: "'Love the Lord your God with all your heart and with all your soul and with all your mind.' [38] This is the first and greatest commandment. [39] And the second is like it: 'Love your neighbor as yourself.' [40] All the Law and the Prophets hang on these two commandments." *Matthew 22:34-40 (NIV)*

If I carry a personal vendetta against the LGBT community, how am I showing my love? I don't see how spreading hate brings people closer to God. It certainly isn't Christ-like.

But the bible teaches homosexuality is a sin, some might say. Irrelevant. My job as a Christian – as a follower of Christ – is to love, not condemn.

> [16] For God so loved the world that he gave his one and only Son, that whoever believes in him shall not perish but have eternal life. [17] For God did not send his Son into the world to condemn the world, but to save the world through him. [18] Whoever believes in him is not condemned, but whoever does not believe stands condemned already because they have not believed in the name of God's one and only Son. [19] This is the verdict: Light has come into the world, but people loved darkness instead of light because their deeds were evil. [20] Everyone who does evil hates the light, and will not come into the light for fear that their deeds will be exposed. [21] But whoever lives by the truth comes into the light, so that it may be seen plainly that what they have done has been done in the sight of God. *John 3:16-21 (NIV)*

Anyone can tell you, I'm not Jesus... not even close. It would be crazy for me to think I'm above him and have the right to judge and condemn others. Truly, the moment I start condemning others is the point I forget what Jesus has done for me. The sacrifice he made on my behalf. I can't consciously deny the gift to another when I know I'm unworthy of it myself.

What about family values? My family has values because we (my husband, in-laws, parents, and I) teach family values to the children. Regardless of what happens outside our home, family values reside within our house. Those family values are centered on following biblical teachings – love and hope rather than hate and condemnation.

Providing equal rights to the LGBT community is no more detrimental to my family than allowing heterosexual couples to divorce and remarry a dozen times. Family values start at home, not in the house of another person.

It's not my place to dictate the lives of others. For one, I have my own family to reign in. I think Jesus says it best:

> [1] "Do not judge, or you too will be judged. [2] For in the same way you judge others, you will be judged, and with the measure you use, it will be measured to you.
>
> [3] "Why do you look at the speck of sawdust in your brother's eye and pay no attention to the plank in your own eye? [4] How can you say to your brother, 'Let me take the speck out of your eye,' when all the time there is a plank in your own eye? [5] You hypocrite, first take the plank out of your own eye, and then you will see clearly to remove the speck from your brother's eye. *Matthew 7:1-5 (NIV)*

I try not to get preachy, but the hatred I see amongst some Christians truly saddens me. What saddens me even more is seeing non-Christians turning away from the faith because of haughty and judgmental attitudes spread by those supposedly walking the righteous life.

If you take nothing else from this message, know that condemnation and spreading hope work against one another. Be a part of the solution, not the problem. Choose today to create a new beginning and spread positive change.

May God fill your live with joy. Black, white, gay, straight, believer or non-believer, God loves you. You are loved.

Special mention goes to Dave Parker at my local PFLAG chapter in NC.

Dave Parker, President
PFLAG Transgender Network
5011 Harness Ln
Colfax, NC 27235-9808
336-285-6088

Made in the USA
Charleston, SC
22 September 2011